FELIX and CALCITE

#1 THE LAND OF THE TROLLS

Artur Laperla

Graphic Universe™ • Minneapolis

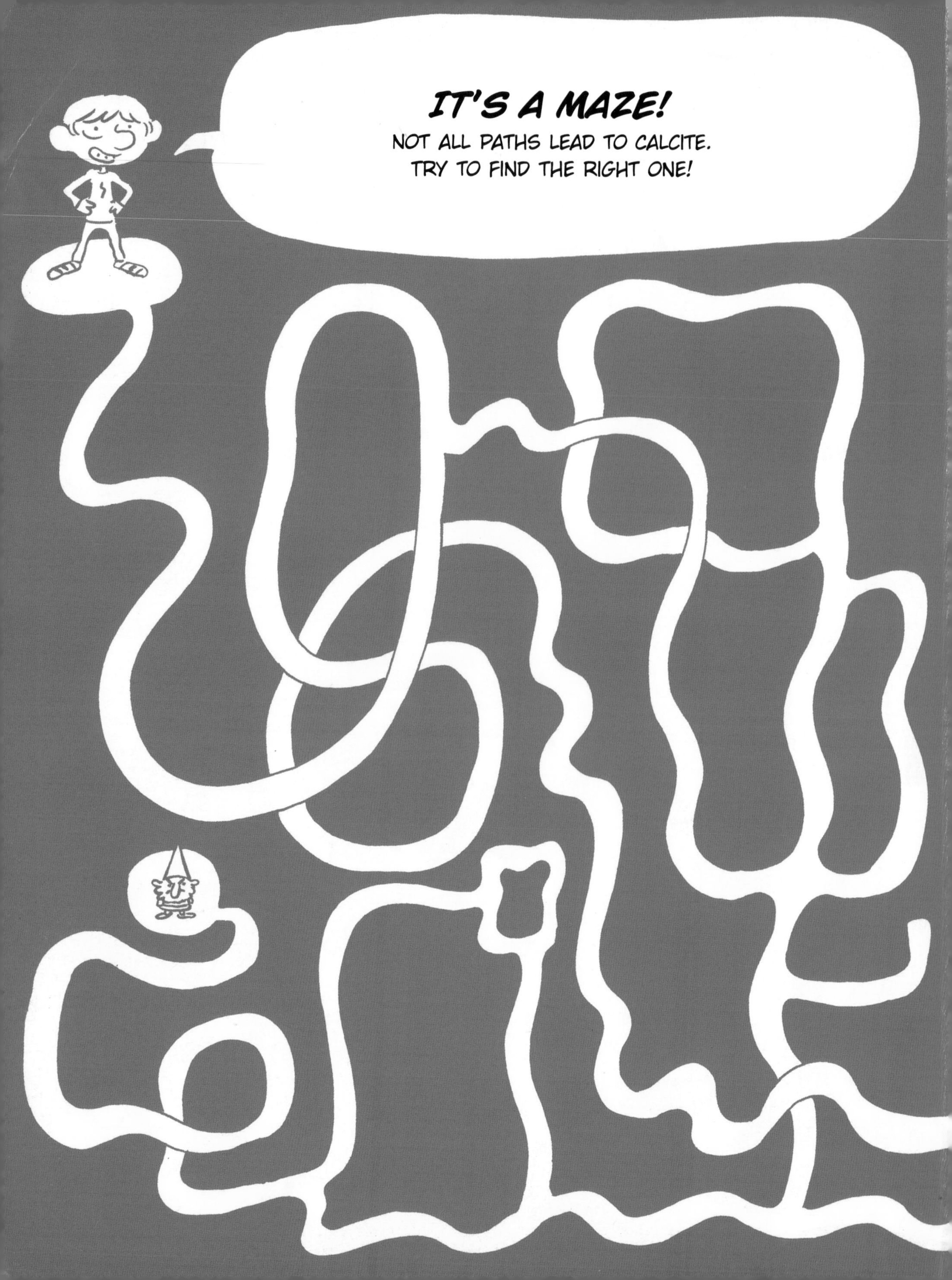
IT'S A MAZE!
NOT ALL PATHS LEAD TO CALCITE.
TRY TO FIND THE RIGHT ONE!

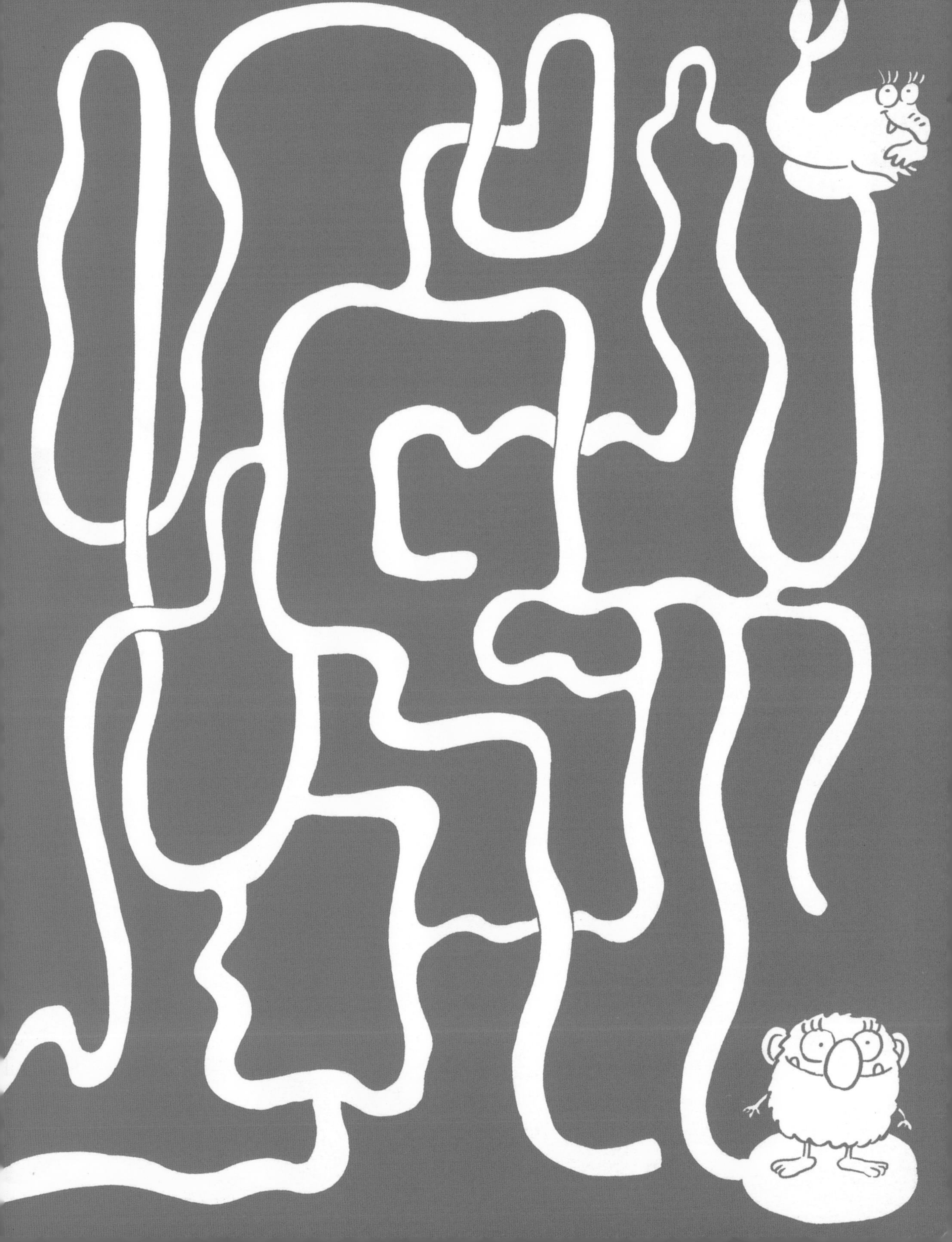

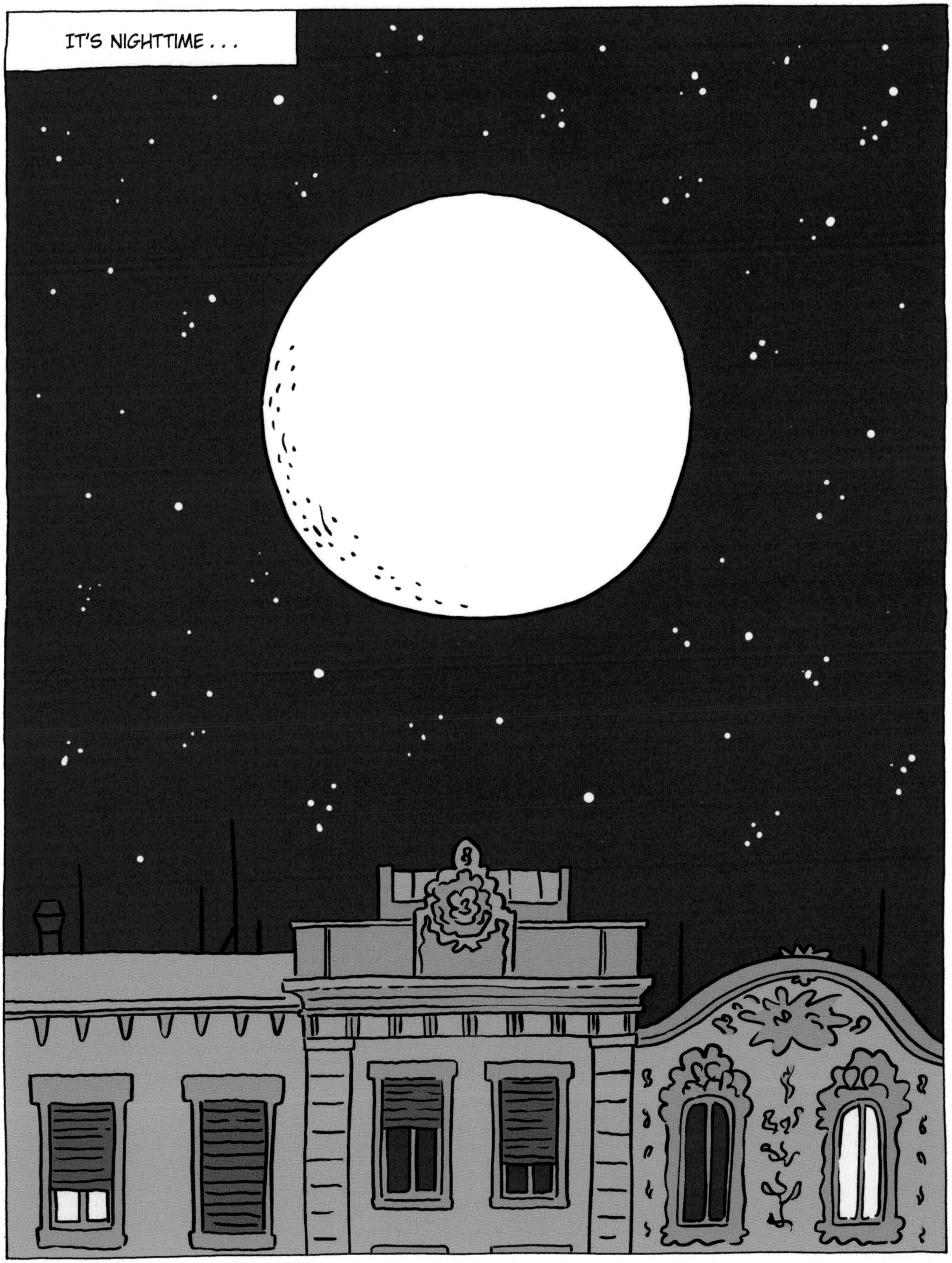
IT'S NIGHTTIME . . .

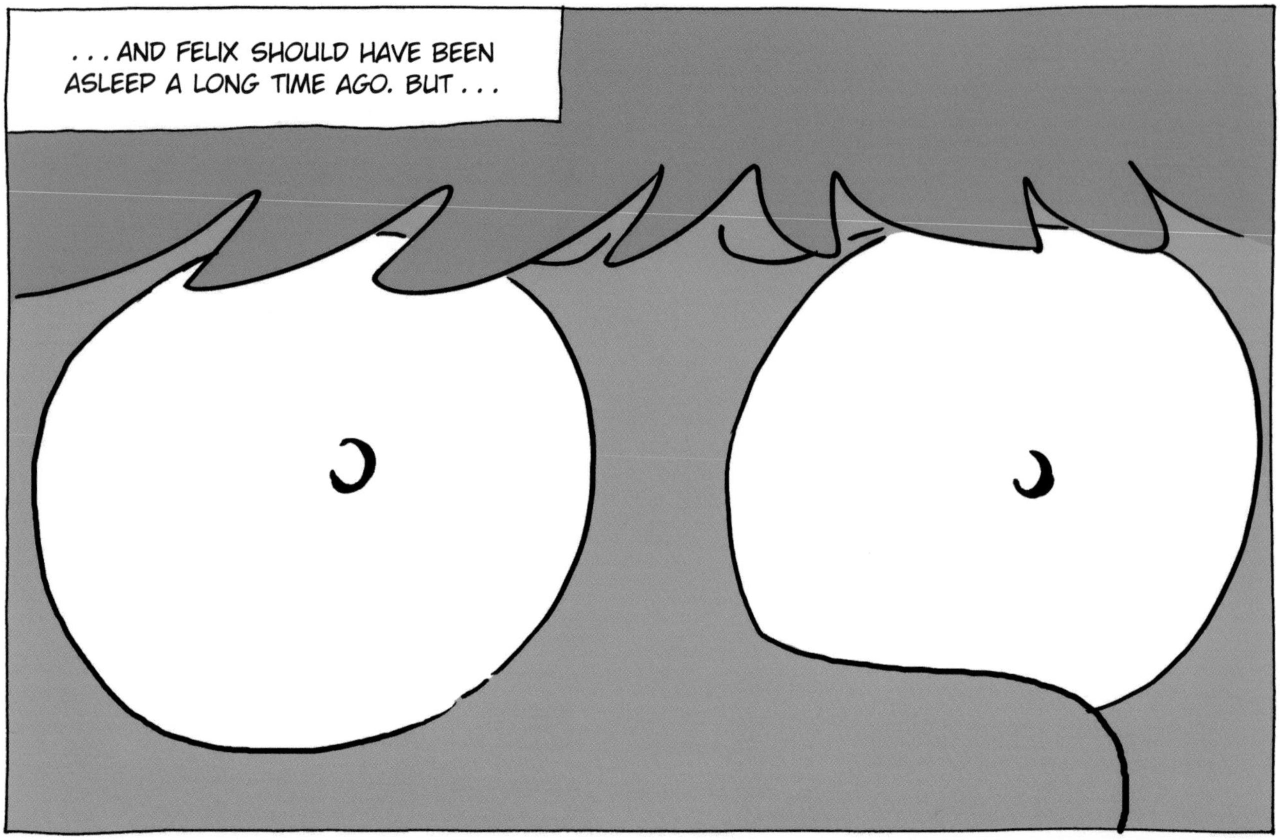
. . . AND FELIX SHOULD HAVE BEEN ASLEEP A LONG TIME AGO. BUT . . .

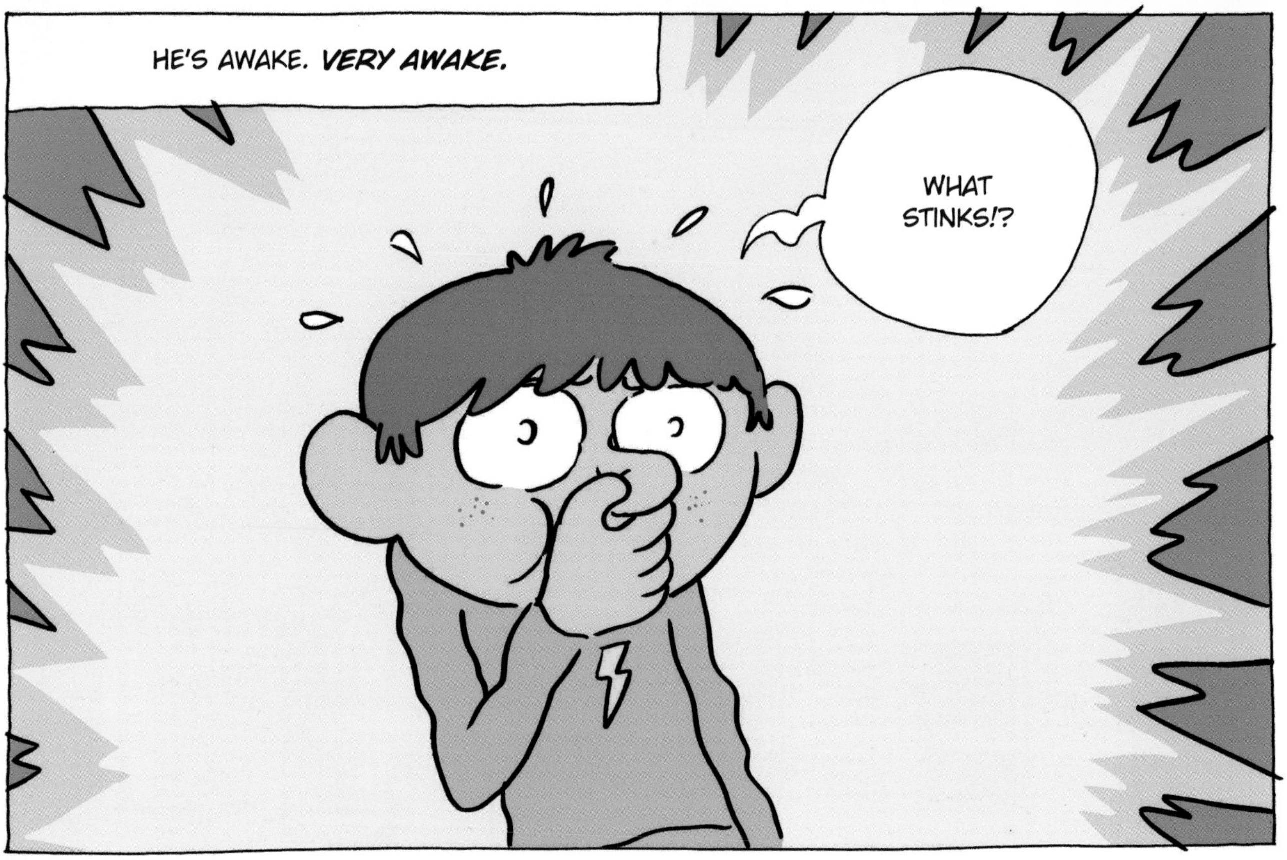
HE'S AWAKE. ***VERY AWAKE.***
WHAT STINKS!?

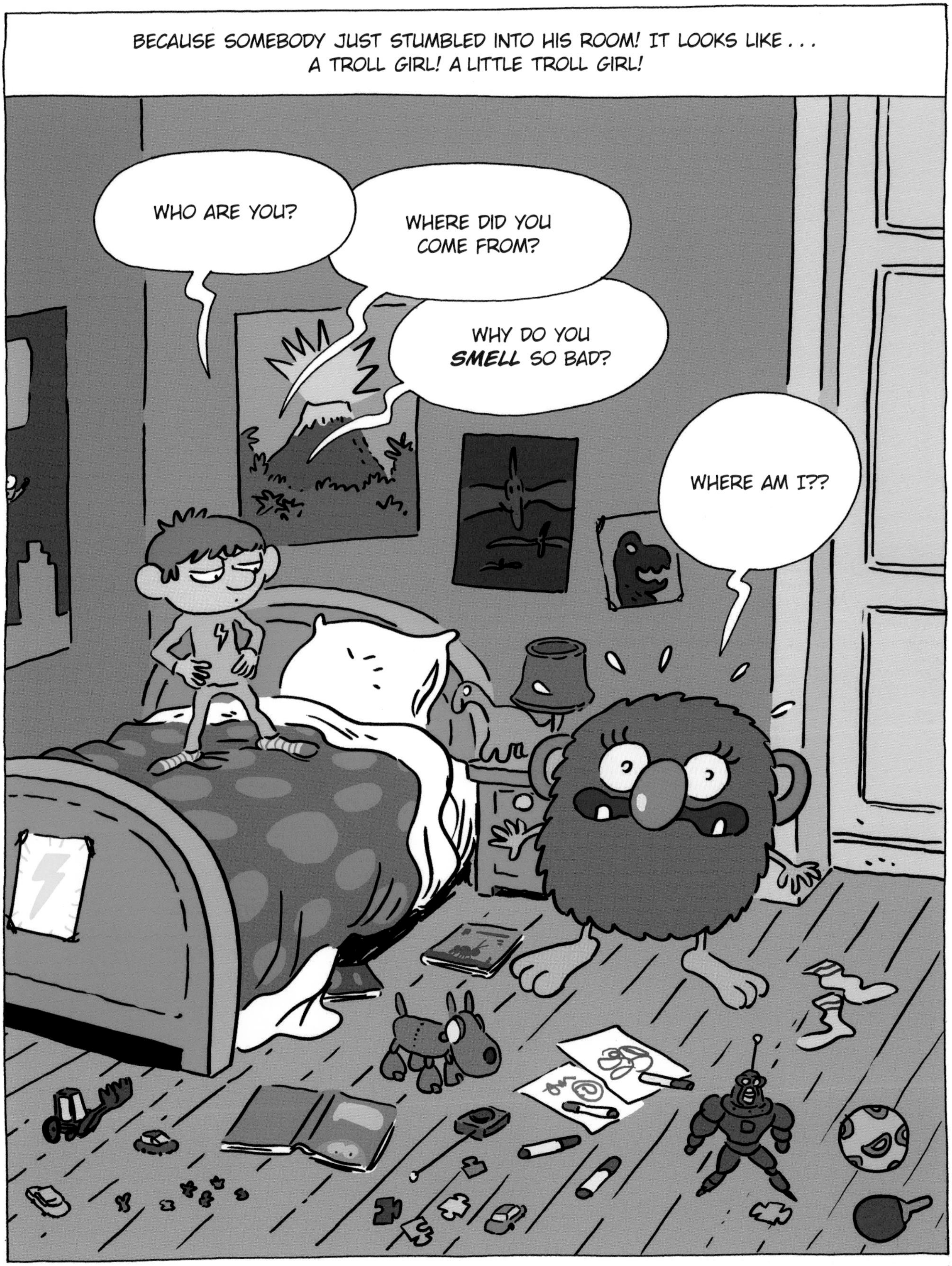
BECAUSE SOMEBODY JUST STUMBLED INTO HIS ROOM! IT LOOKS LIKE . . .
A TROLL GIRL! A LITTLE TROLL GIRL!
WHO ARE YOU?
WHERE DID YOU COME FROM?
WHY DO YOU **SMELL** SO BAD?
WHERE AM I??

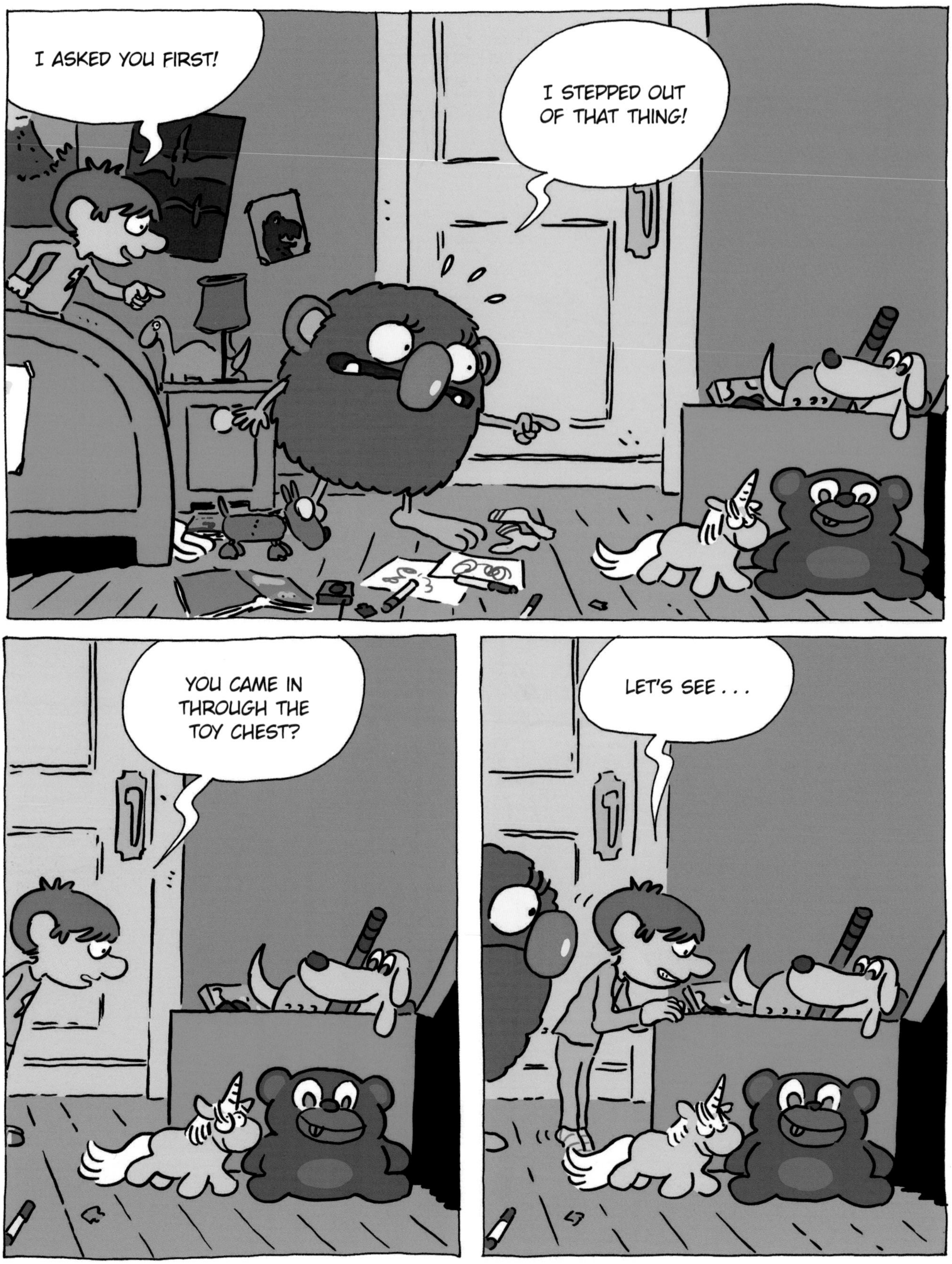
I ASKED YOU FIRST!
I STEPPED OUT OF THAT THING!
YOU CAME IN THROUGH THE TOY CHEST?
LET'S SEE . . .

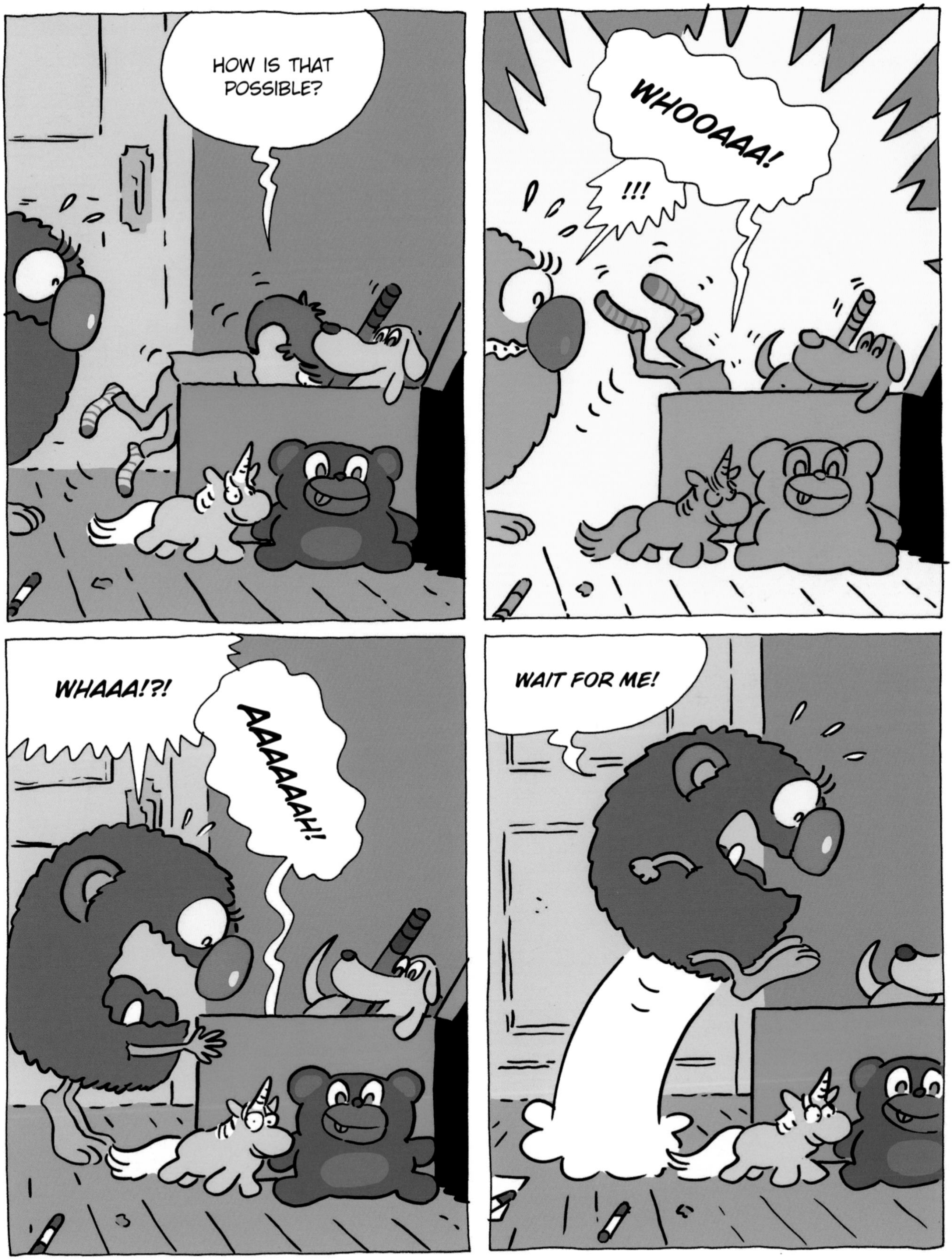
HOW IS THAT POSSIBLE?
WHOOAAA!
!!!
WHAAA!?!
AAAAAAAH!
WAIT FOR ME!

QUICK! TURN YOUR
BOOK TO THE RIGHT.

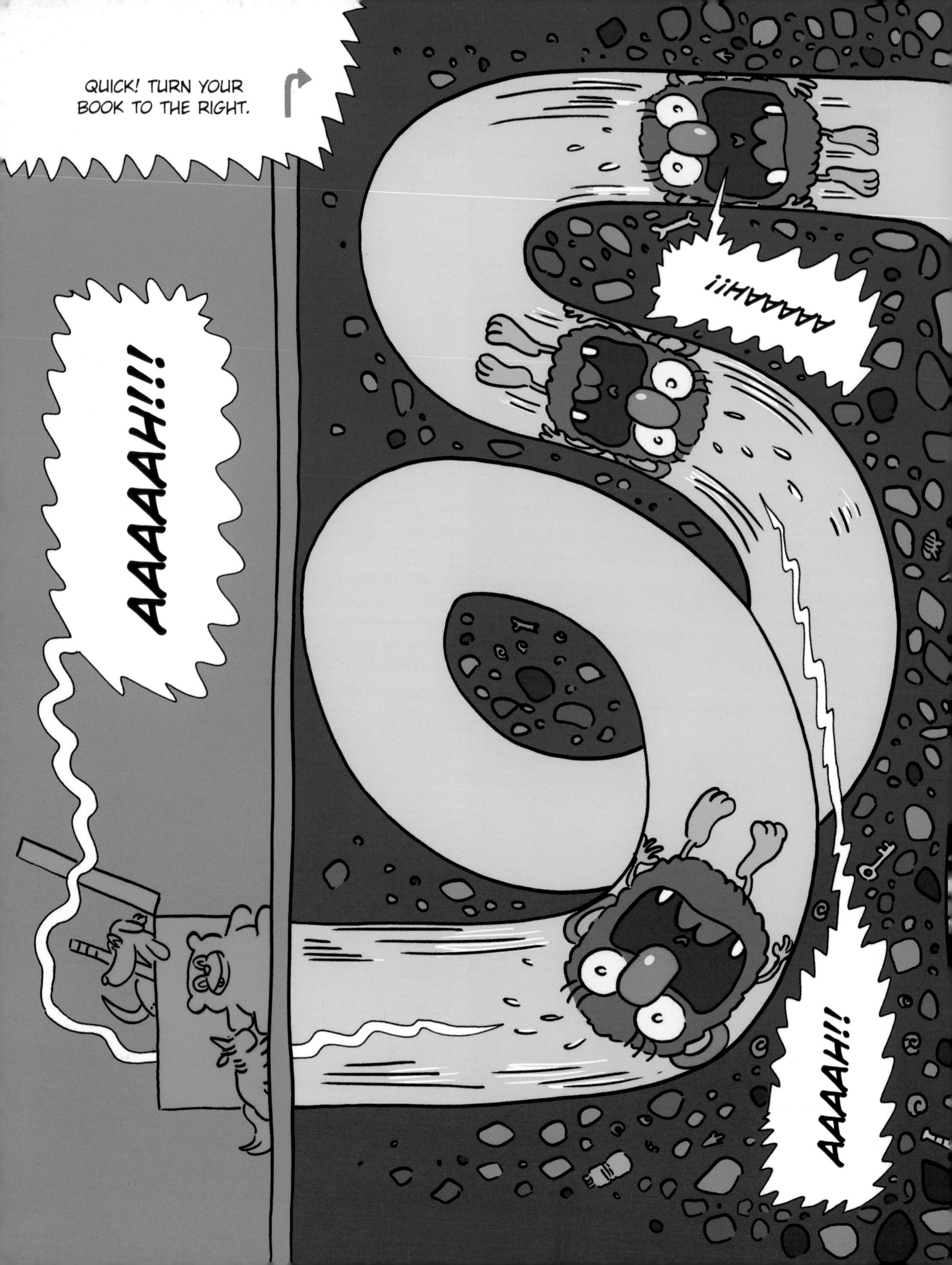

AAAAAAH!!!!
AAAAH!!
AAAAAH!!

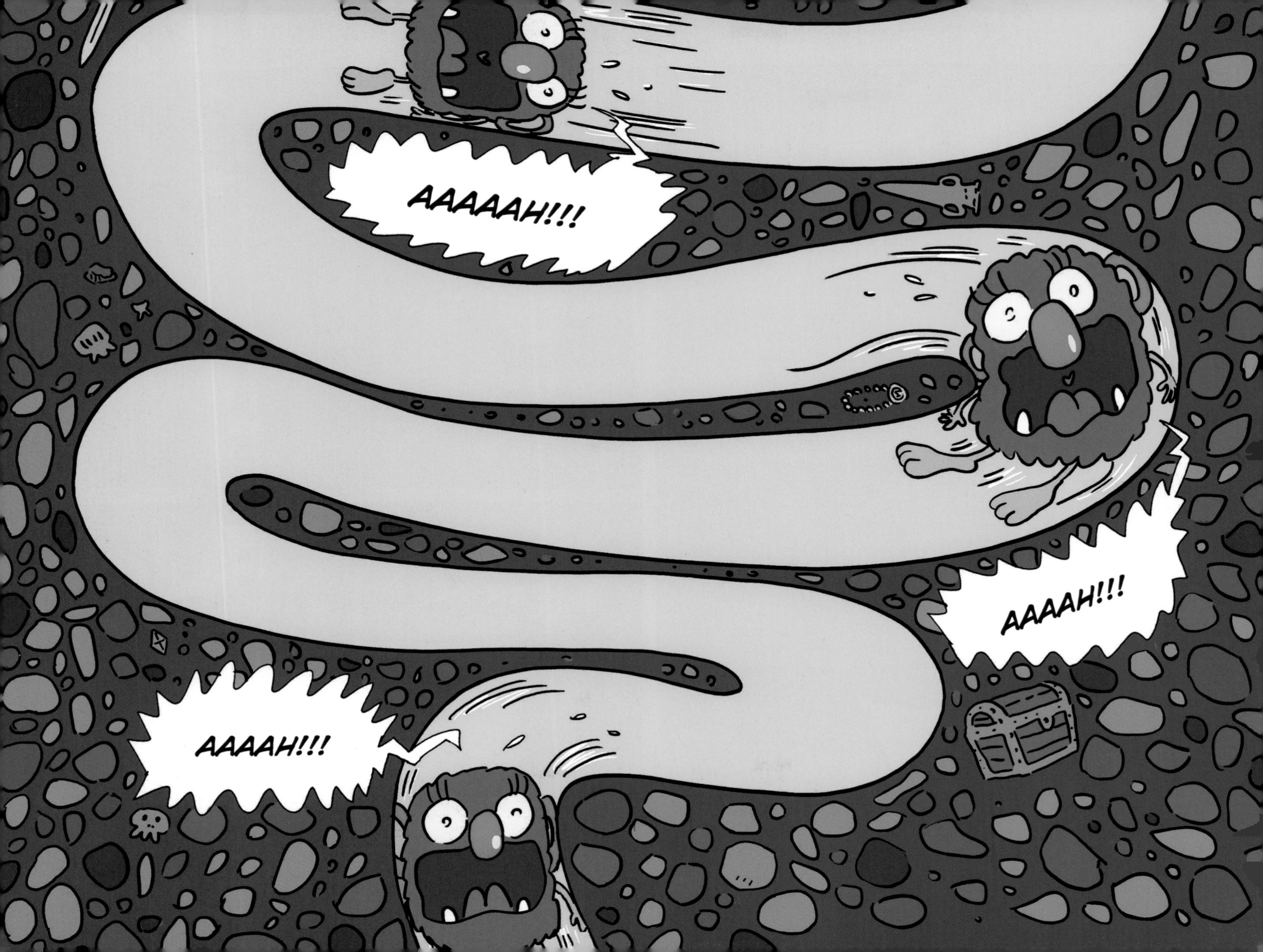
AAAAAH!!!
AAAAH!!!
AAAAH!!!

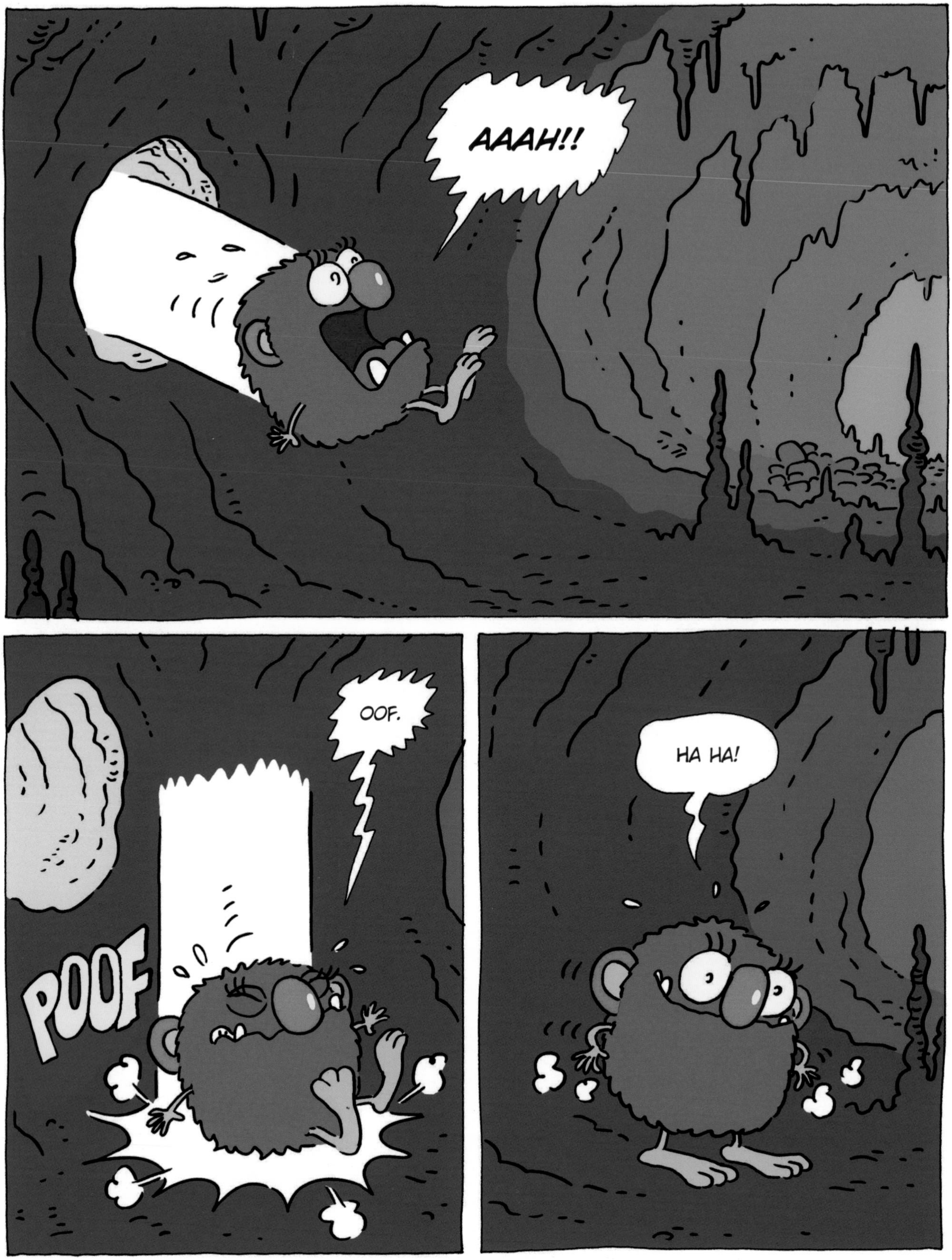
AAAH!!
OOF.
POOF
HA HA!

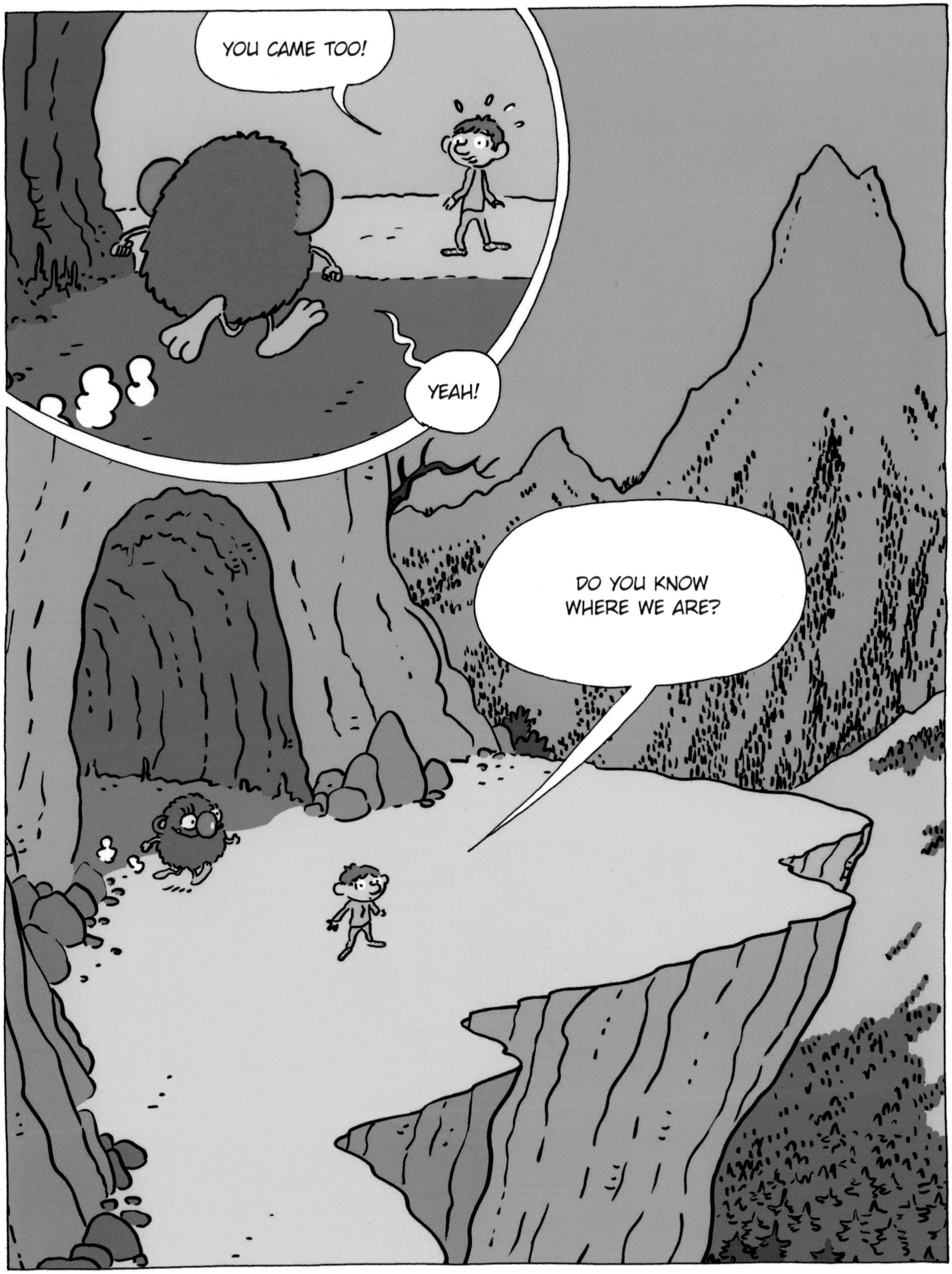
YOU CAME TOO!
YEAH!
DO YOU KNOW WHERE WE ARE?

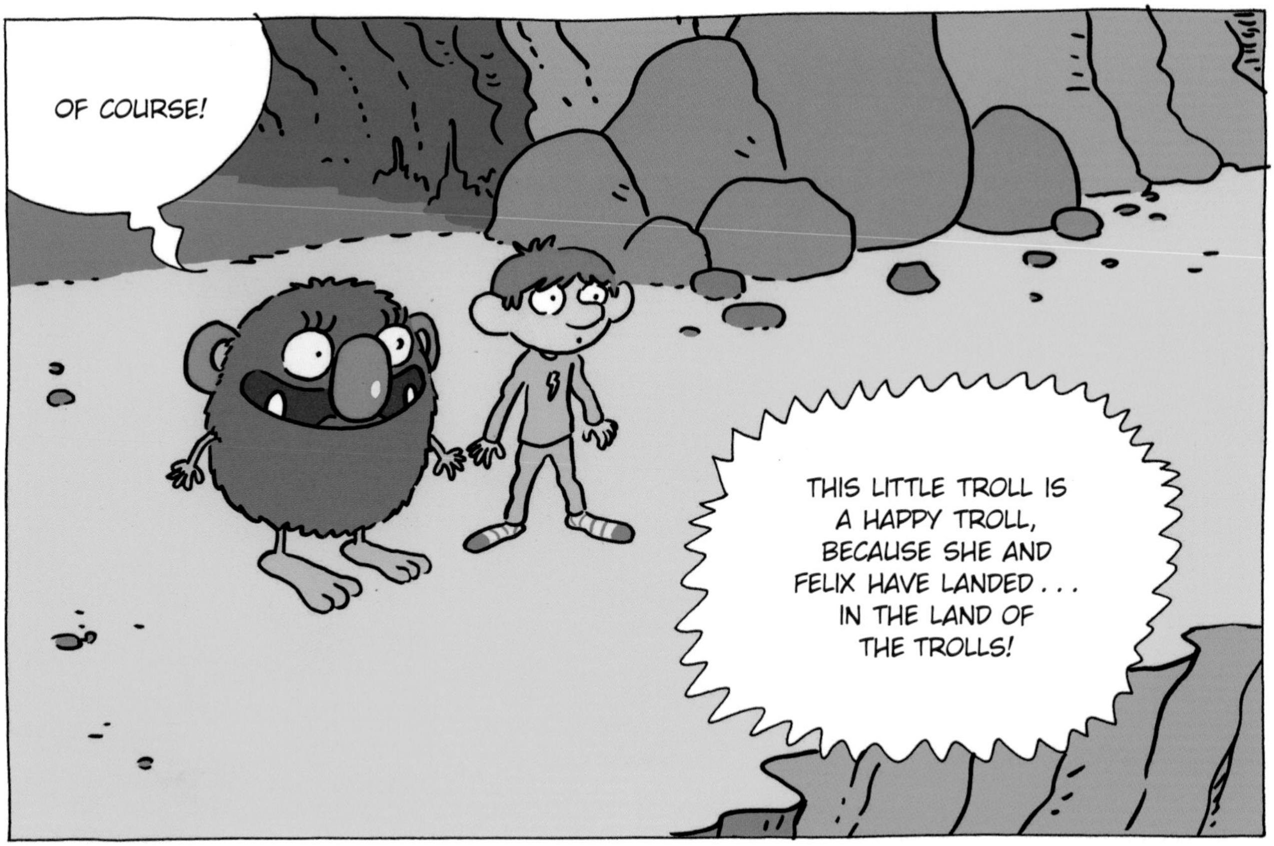
OF COURSE!
THIS LITTLE TROLL IS A HAPPY TROLL, BECAUSE SHE AND FELIX HAVE LANDED . . . IN THE LAND OF THE TROLLS!

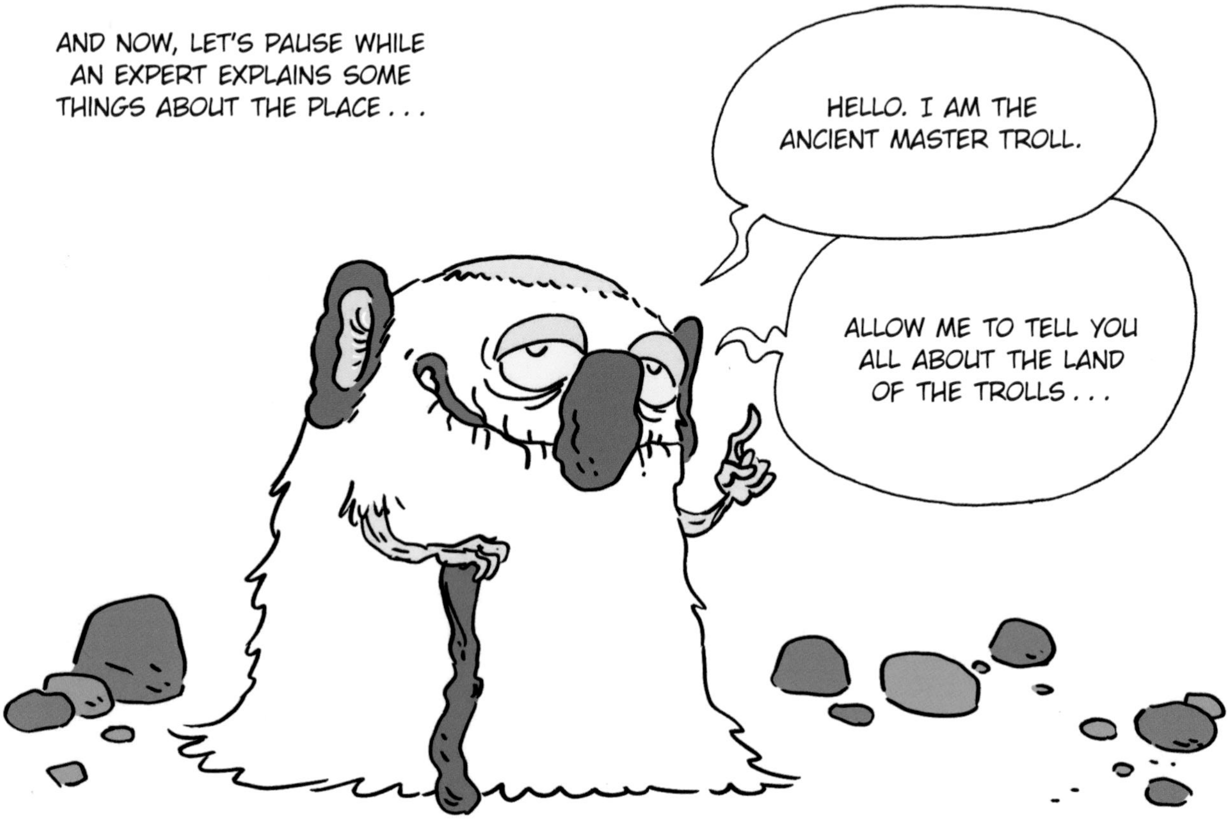
AND NOW, LET'S PAUSE WHILE AN EXPERT EXPLAINS SOME THINGS ABOUT THE PLACE . . .
HELLO. I AM THE ANCIENT MASTER TROLL.
ALLOW ME TO TELL YOU ALL ABOUT THE LAND OF THE TROLLS . . .

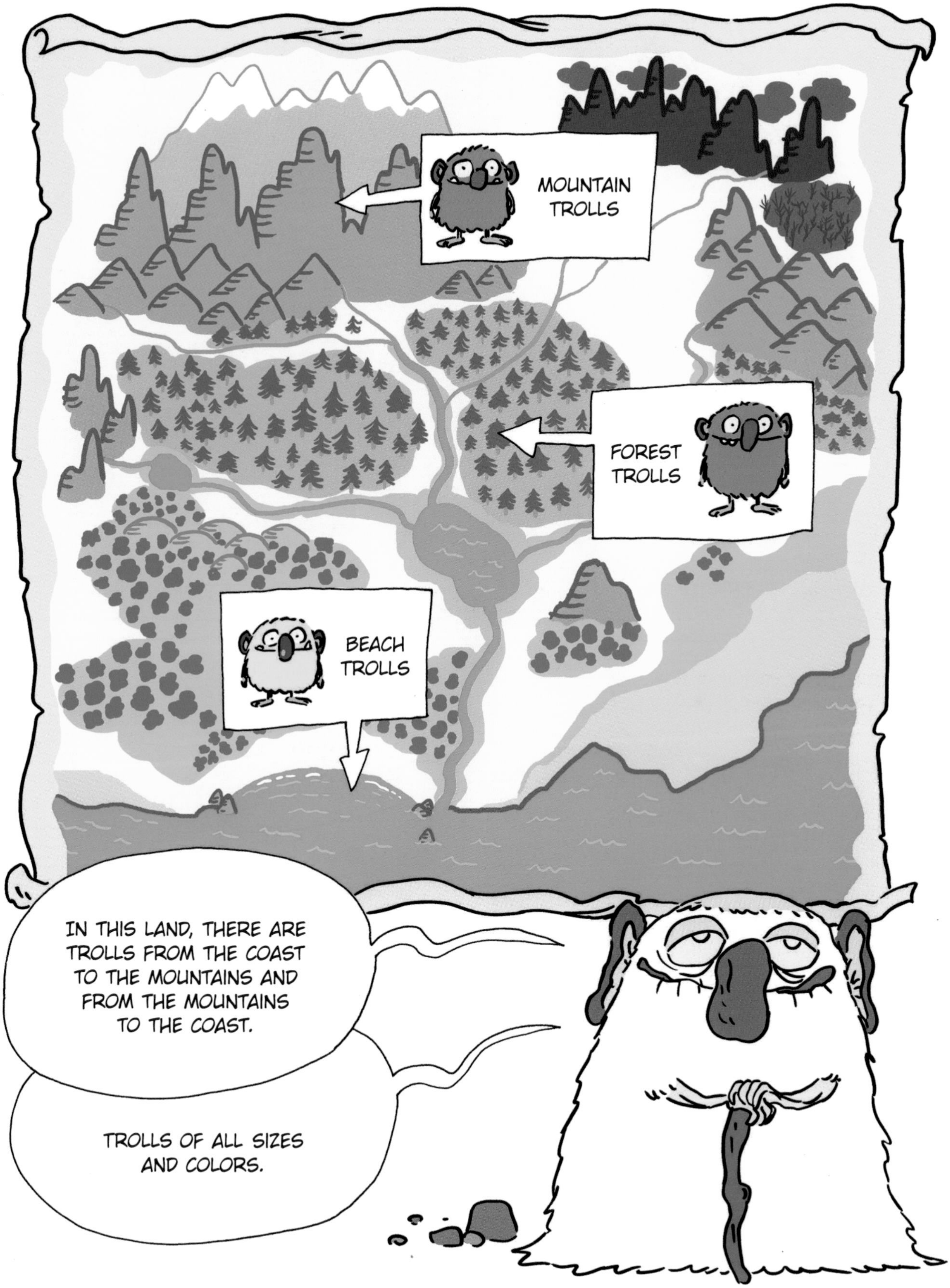
MOUNTAIN TROLLS
FOREST TROLLS
BEACH TROLLS
IN THIS LAND, THERE ARE TROLLS FROM THE COAST TO THE MOUNTAINS AND FROM THE MOUNTAINS TO THE COAST.
TROLLS OF ALL SIZES AND COLORS.

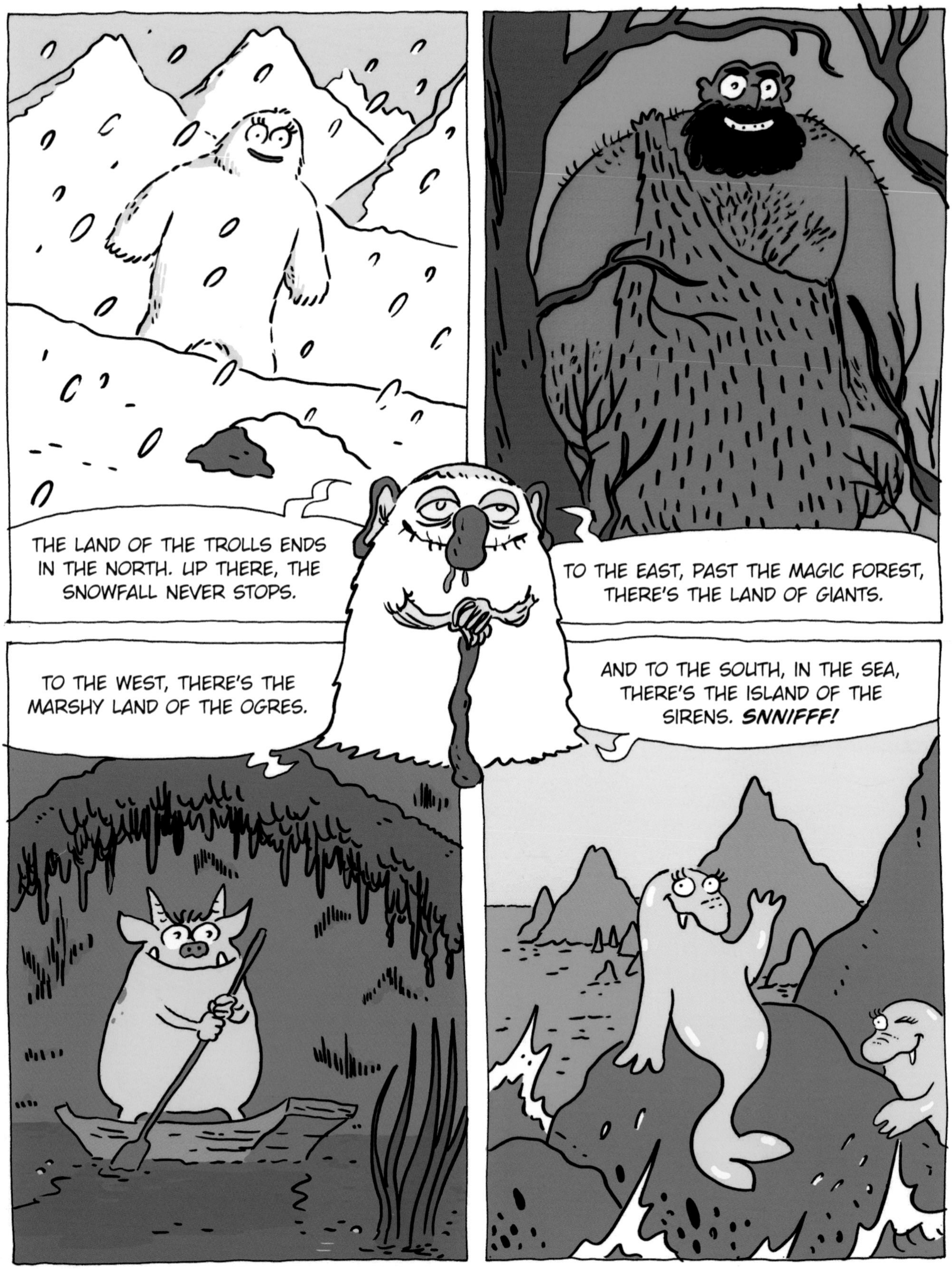
THE LAND OF THE TROLLS ENDS IN THE NORTH. UP THERE, THE SNOWFALL NEVER STOPS.
TO THE EAST, PAST THE MAGIC FOREST, THERE'S THE LAND OF GIANTS.
TO THE WEST, THERE'S THE MARSHY LAND OF THE OGRES.
AND TO THE SOUTH, IN THE SEA, THERE'S THE ISLAND OF THE SIRENS. **SNNIFFF!**

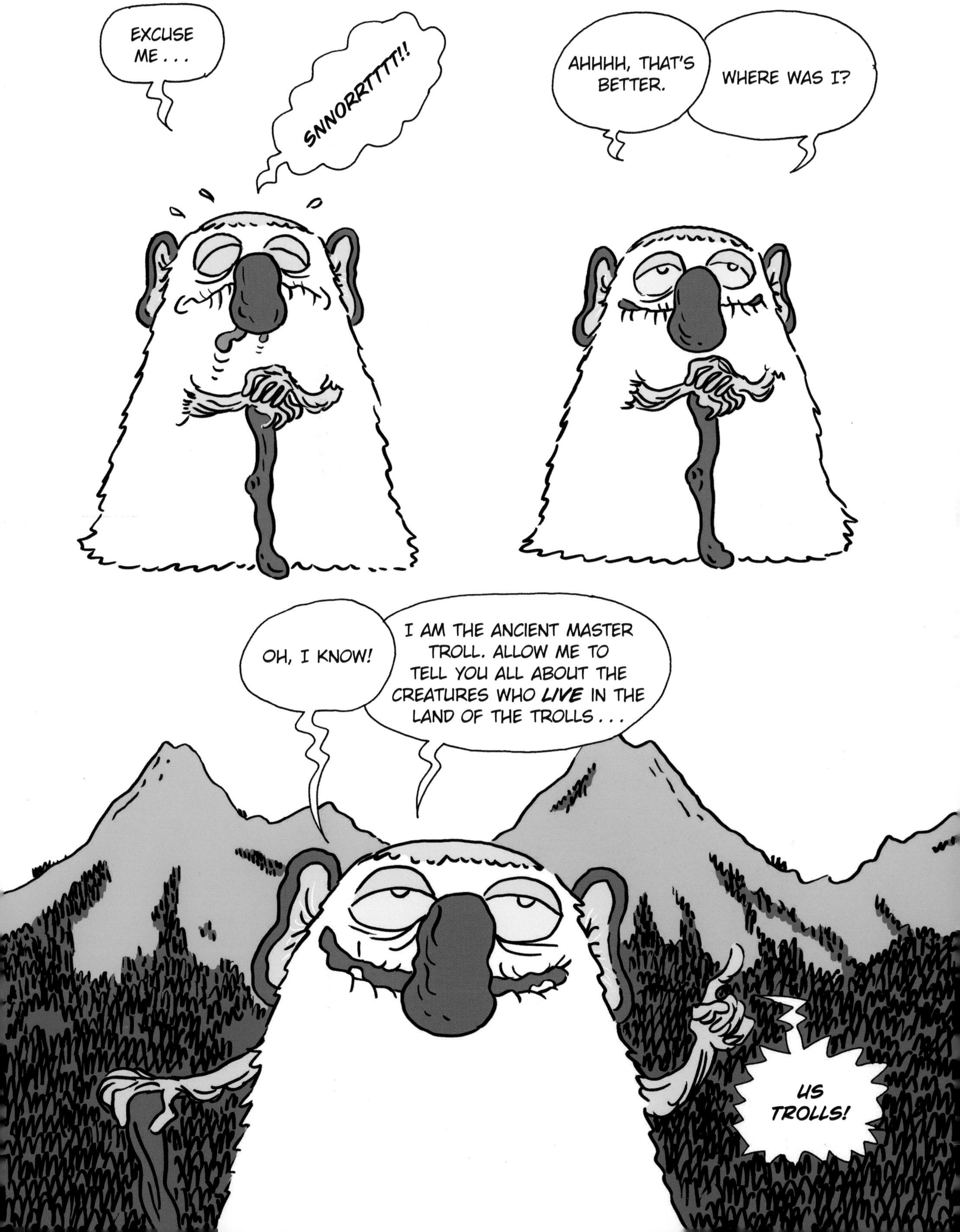
EXCUSE ME . . .
SNNORRTTTT!!
AHHHH, THAT'S BETTER.
WHERE WAS I?
OH, I KNOW!
I AM THE ANCIENT MASTER TROLL. ALLOW ME TO TELL YOU ALL ABOUT THE CREATURES WHO LIVE IN THE LAND OF THE TROLLS . . .
US TROLLS!

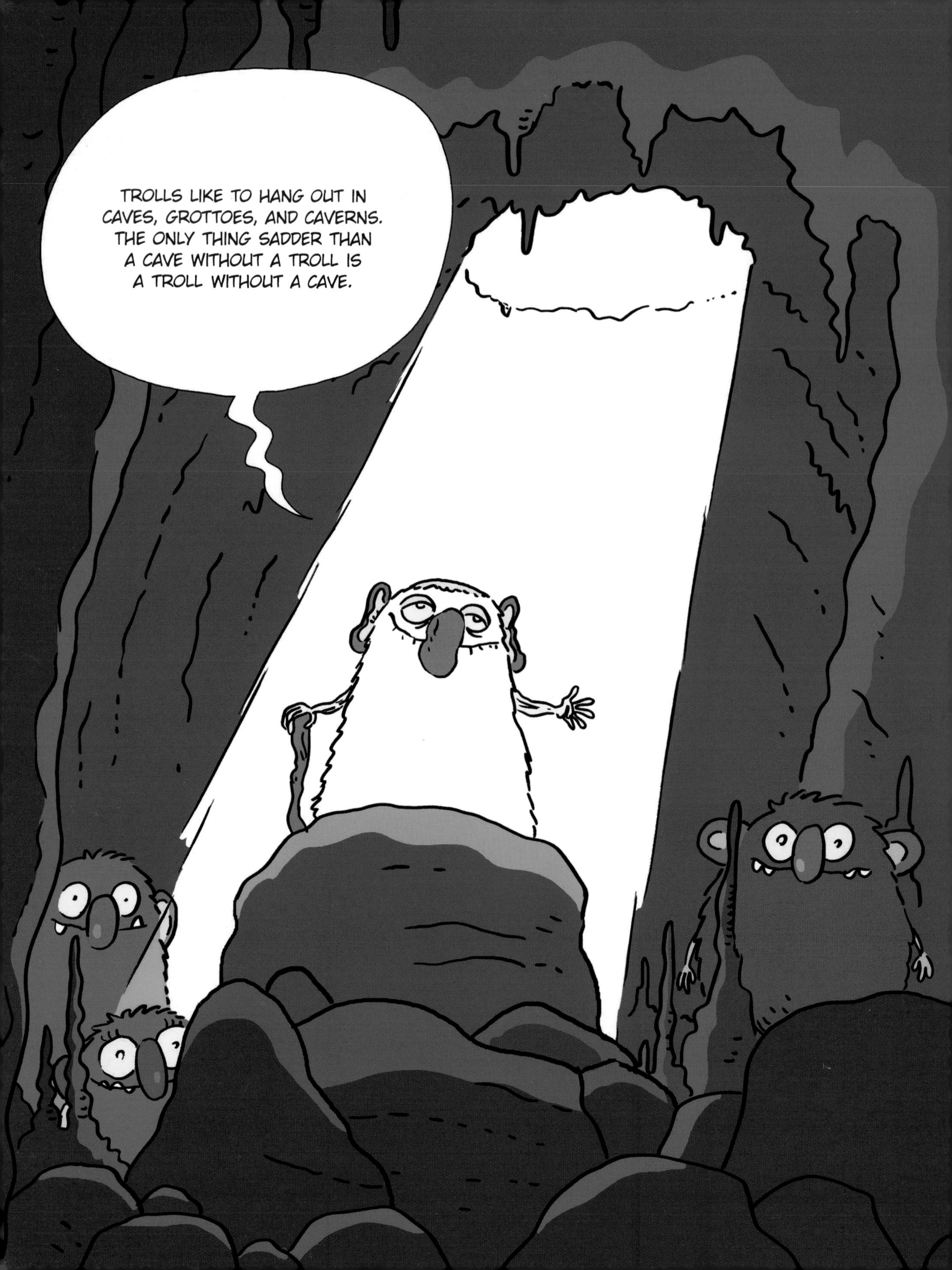
TROLLS LIKE TO HANG OUT IN CAVES, GROTTOES, AND CAVERNS. THE ONLY THING SADDER THAN A CAVE WITHOUT A TROLL IS A TROLL WITHOUT A CAVE.

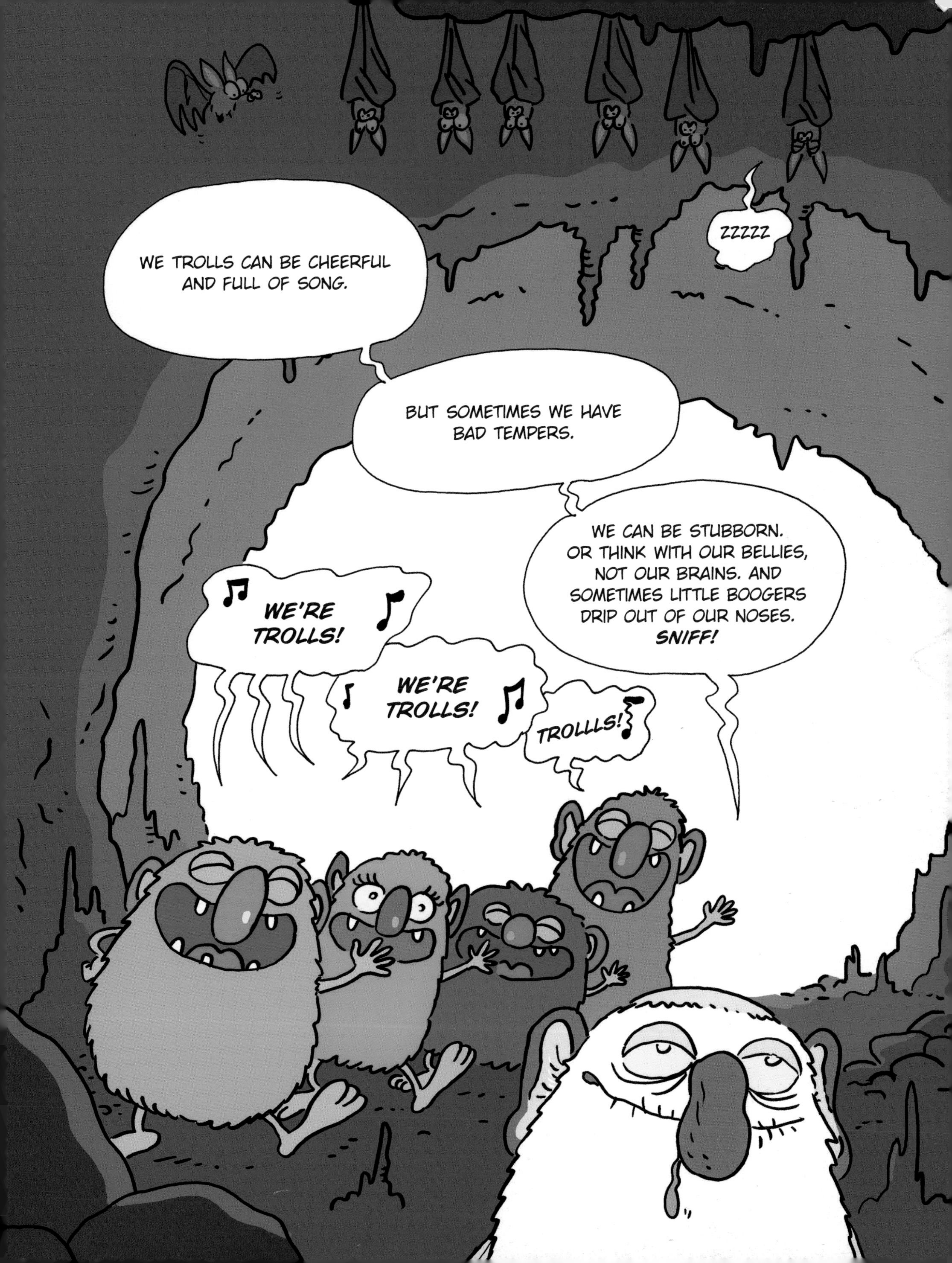
ZZZZZ
WE TROLLS CAN BE CHEERFUL AND FULL OF SONG.
BUT SOMETIMES WE HAVE BAD TEMPERS.
WE CAN BE STUBBORN. OR THINK WITH OUR BELLIES, NOT OUR BRAINS. AND SOMETIMES LITTLE BOOGERS DRIP OUT OF OUR NOSES. SNIFF!
WE'RE TROLLS!
WE'RE TROLLS!
TROLLLS!

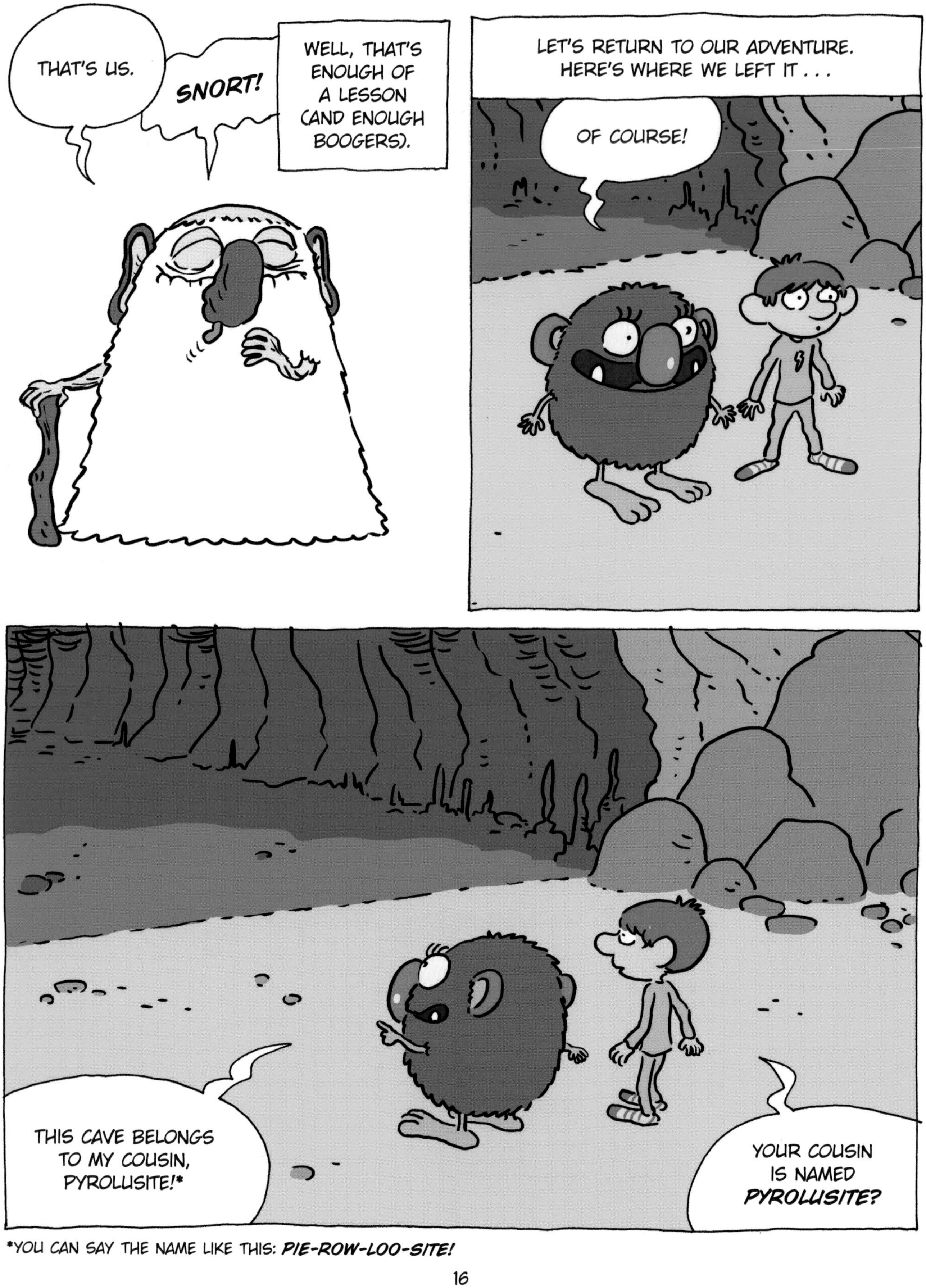
THAT'S US.
SNORT!
WELL, THAT'S ENOUGH OF A LESSON (AND ENOUGH BOOGERS).
LET'S RETURN TO OUR ADVENTURE. HERE'S WHERE WE LEFT IT . . .
OF COURSE!
THIS CAVE BELONGS TO MY COUSIN, PYROLUSITE!*
YOUR COUSIN IS NAMED *PYROLUSITE?*

*YOU CAN SAY THE NAME LIKE THIS: ***PIE-ROW-LOO-SITE!***

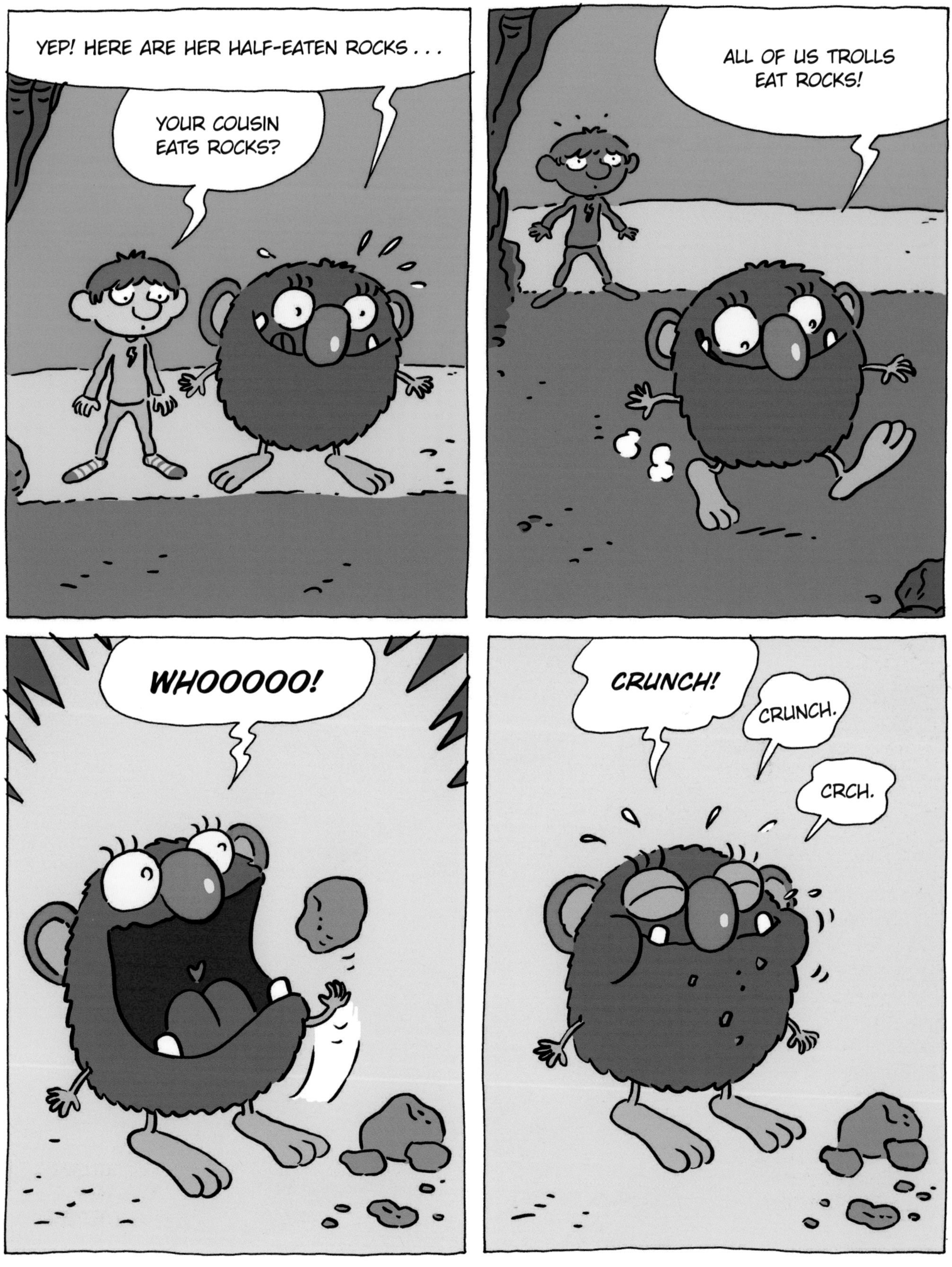
YEP! HERE ARE HER HALF-EATEN ROCKS . . .
YOUR COUSIN EATS ROCKS?
ALL OF US TROLLS EAT ROCKS!
WHOOOOO!
CRUNCH!
CRUNCH.
CRCH.

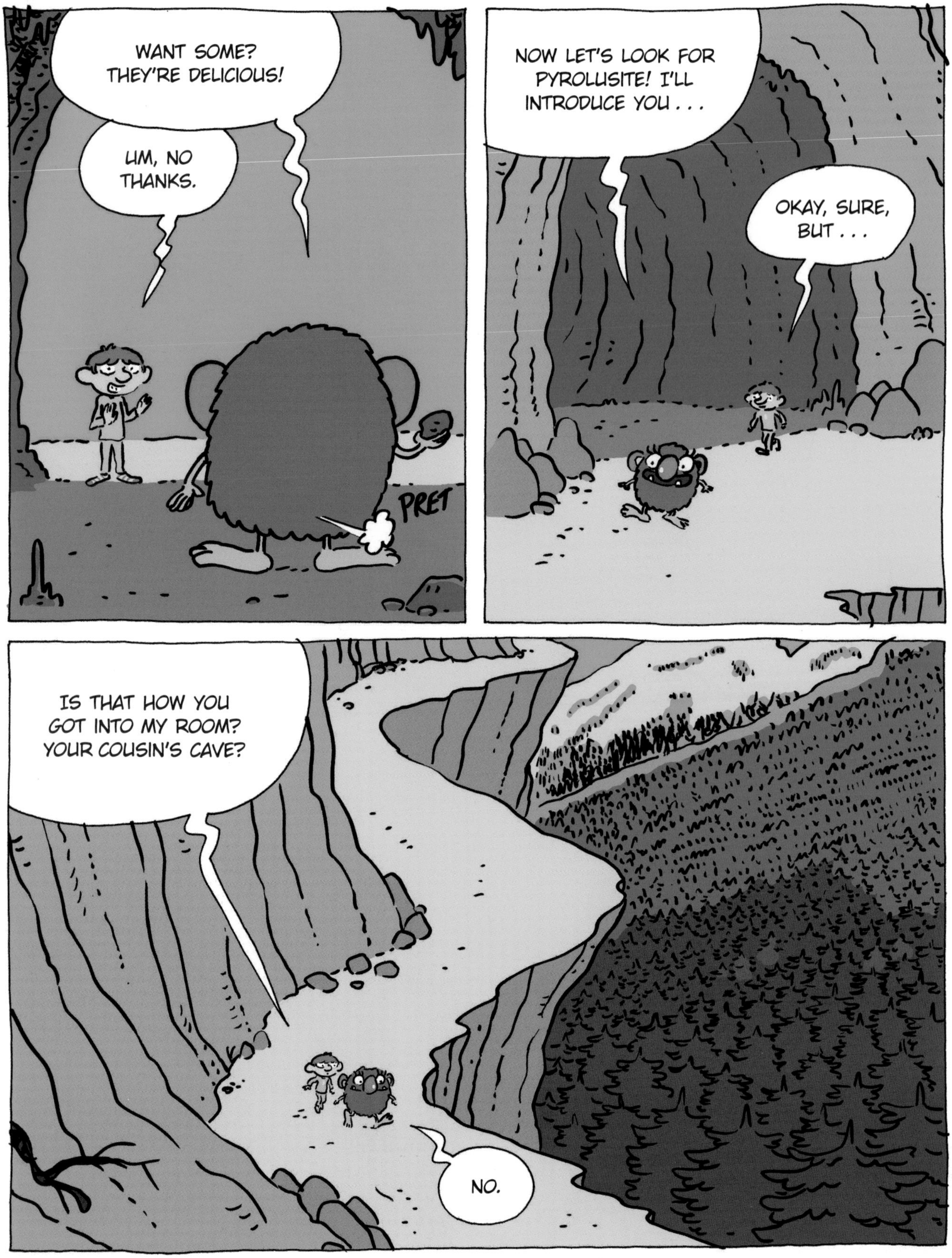
WANT SOME? THEY'RE DELICIOUS!
UM, NO THANKS.
PRET
NOW LET'S LOOK FOR PYROLUSITE! I'LL INTRODUCE YOU . . .
OKAY, SURE, BUT . . .
IS THAT HOW YOU GOT INTO MY ROOM? YOUR COUSIN'S CAVE?
NO.

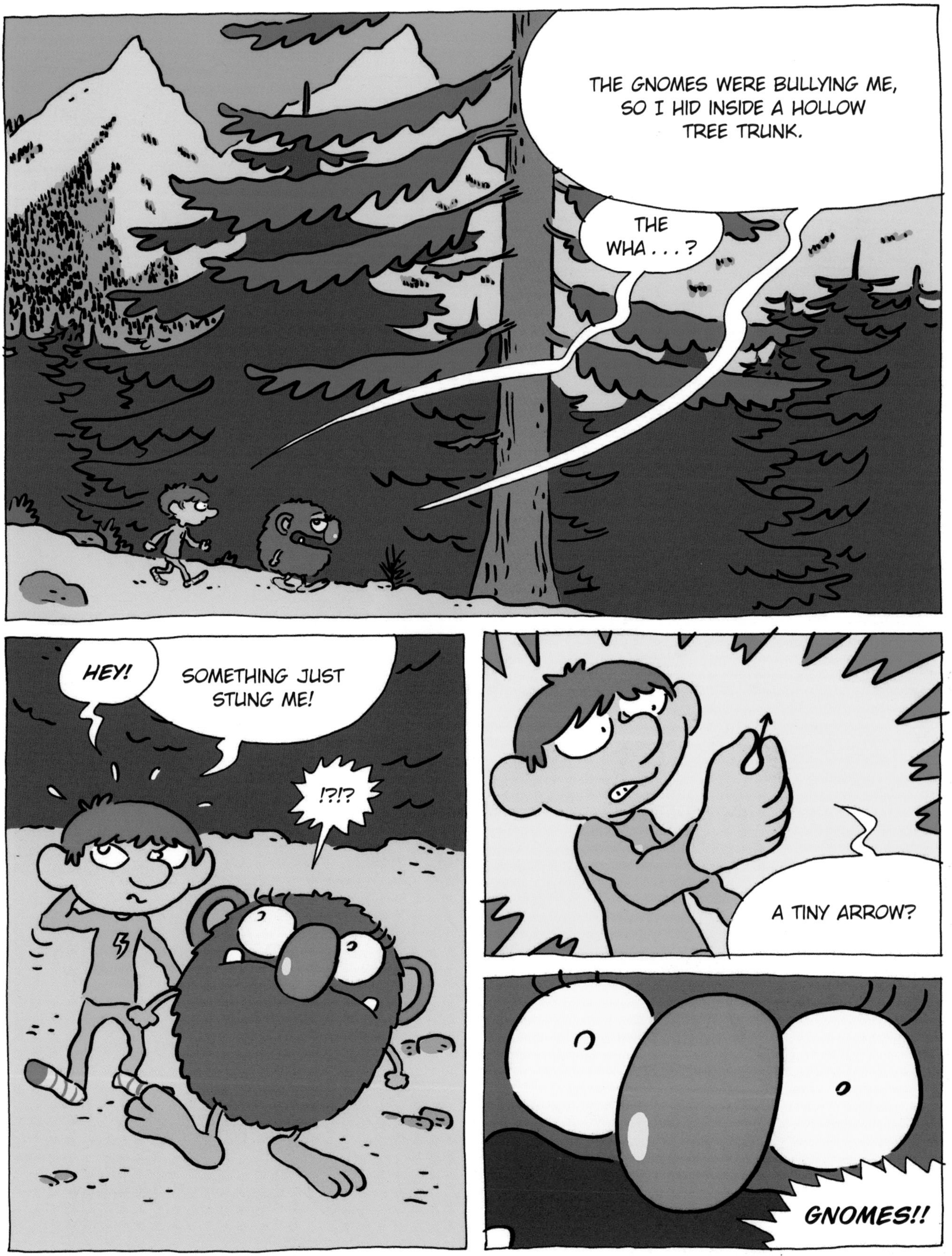
THE GNOMES WERE BULLYING ME, SO I HID INSIDE A HOLLOW TREE TRUNK.
THE WHA . . . ?
HEY!
SOMETHING JUST STUNG ME!
!?!?
A TINY ARROW?
GNOMES!!

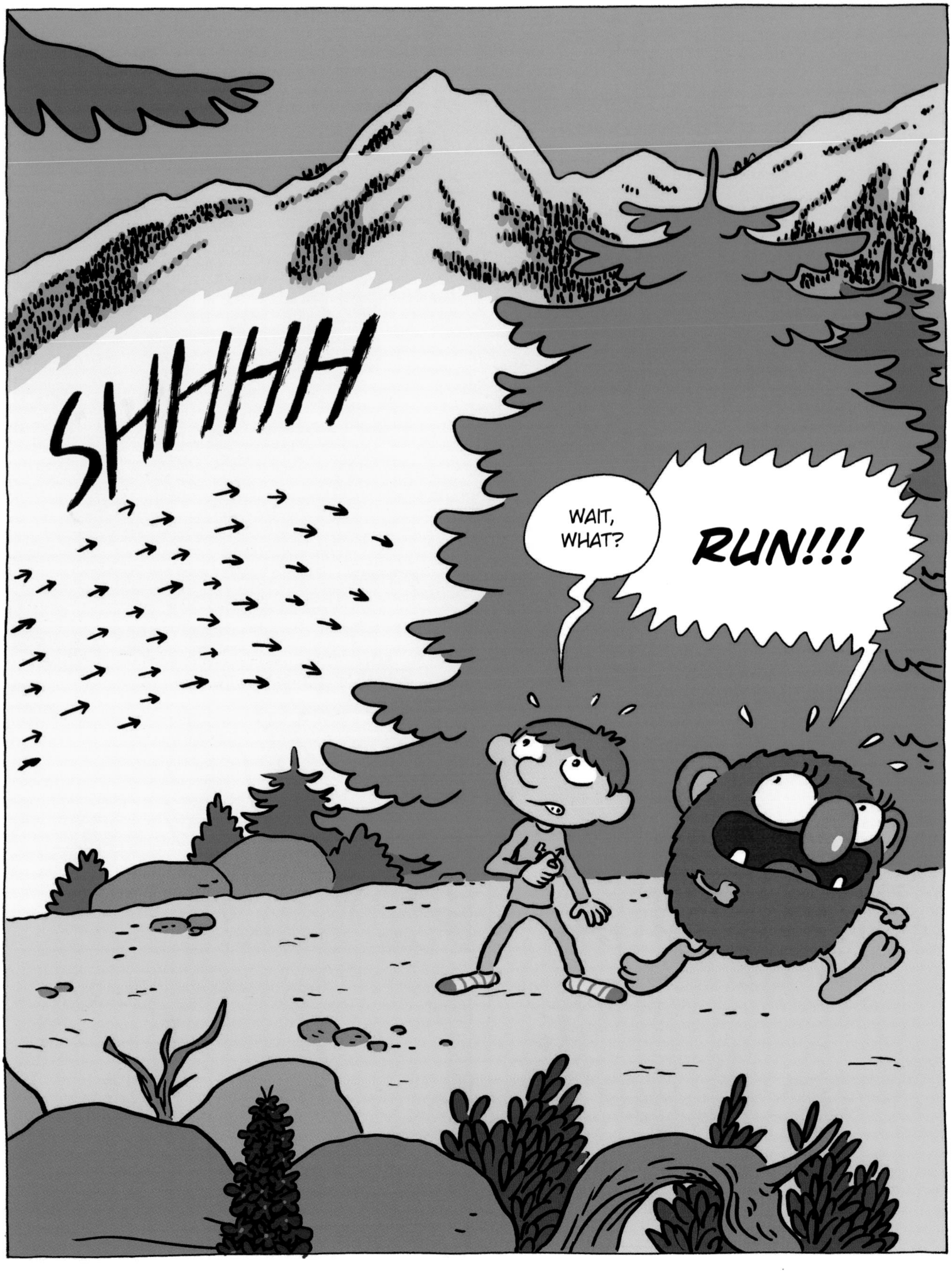
SHHHH
WAIT, WHAT?
RUN!!!

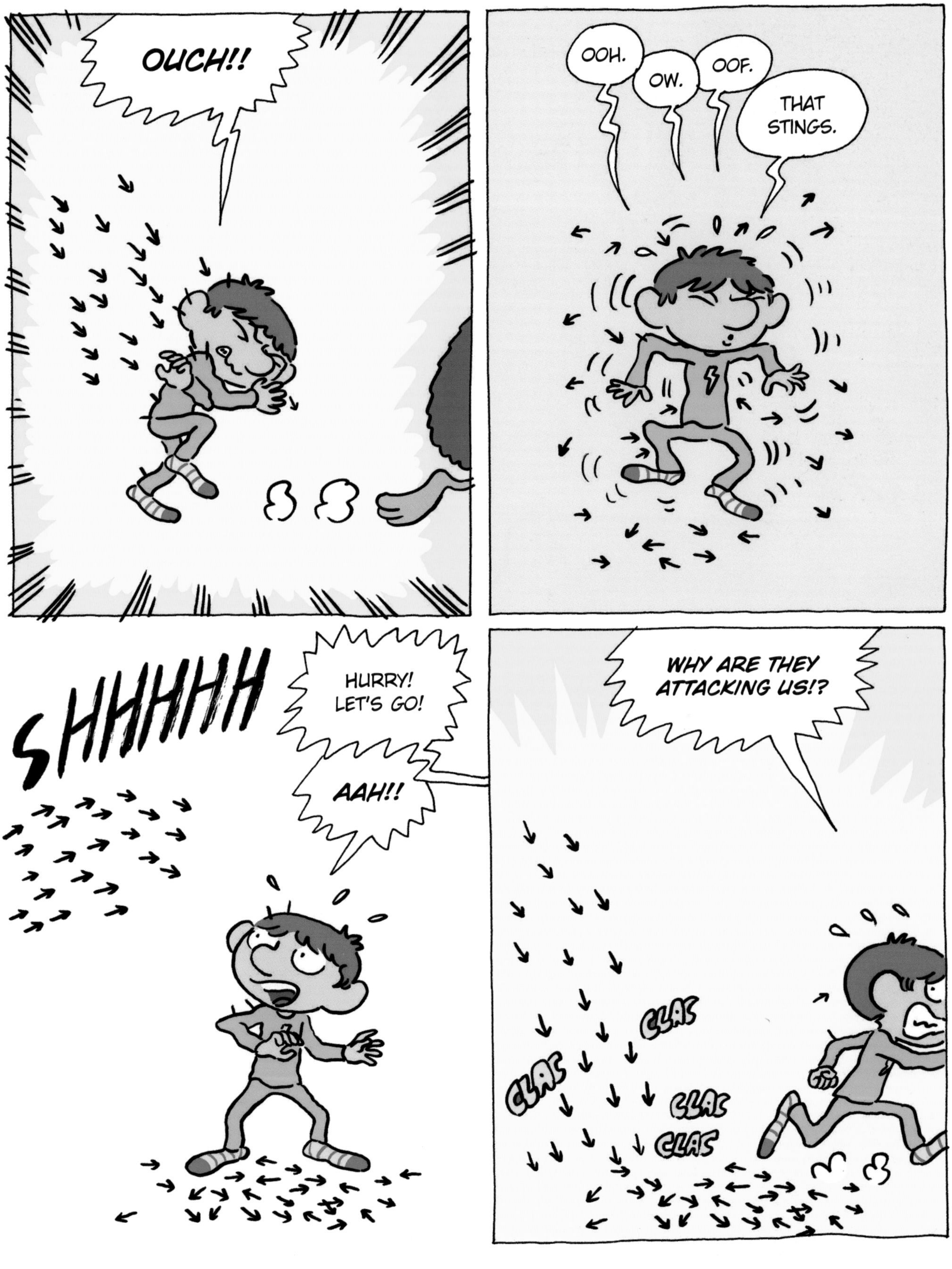
OUCH!!
OOH.
OW.
OOF.
THAT STINGS.
SHHHHHH
HURRY! LET'S GO!
AAH!!
WHY ARE THEY ATTACKING US!?
CLAC
CLAC
CLAC
CLAC

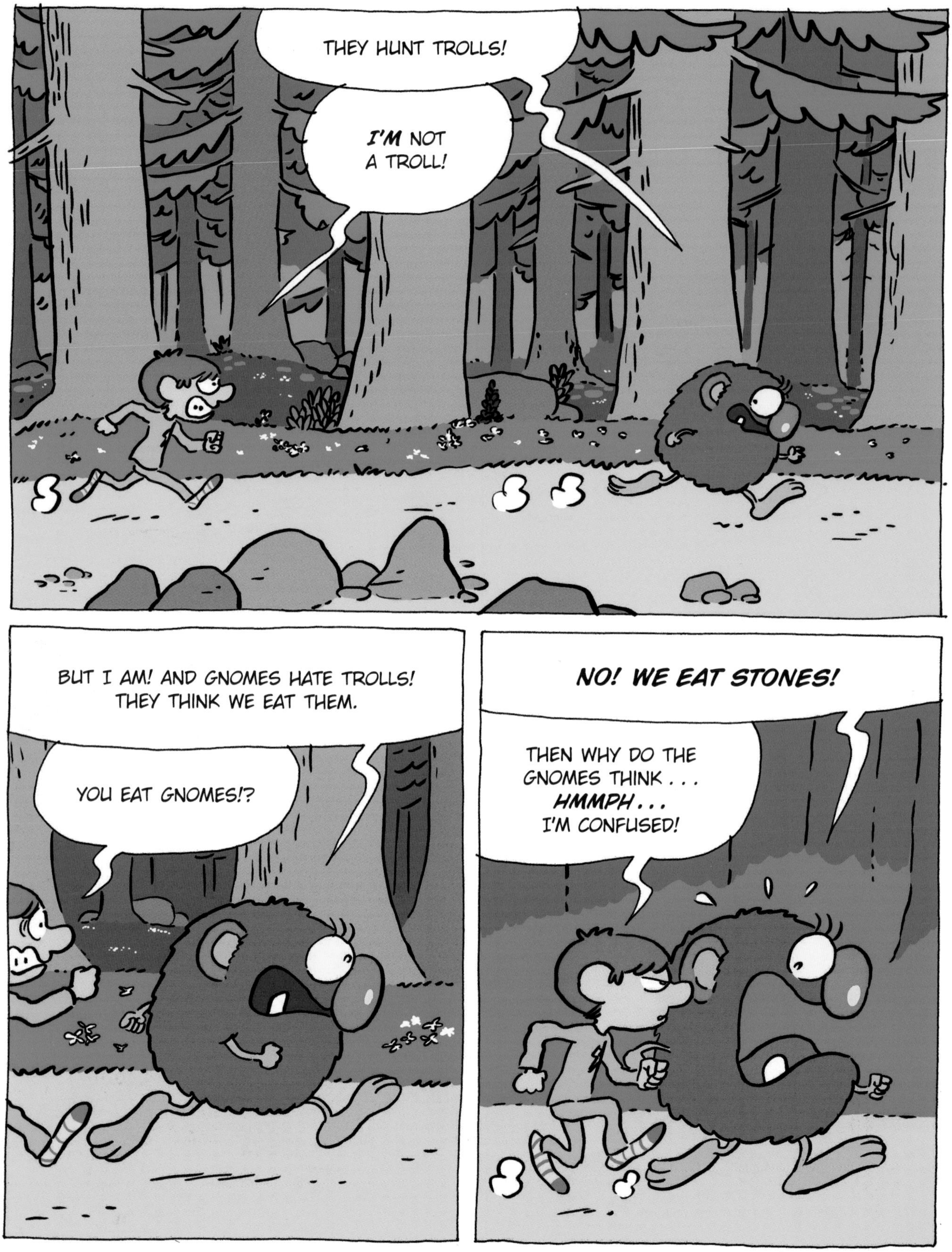
THEY HUNT TROLLS!
I'M NOT A TROLL!
BUT I AM! AND GNOMES HATE TROLLS! THEY THINK WE EAT THEM.
YOU EAT GNOMES!?
NO! WE EAT STONES!
THEN WHY DO THE GNOMES THINK . . . HMMPH . . . I'M CONFUSED!

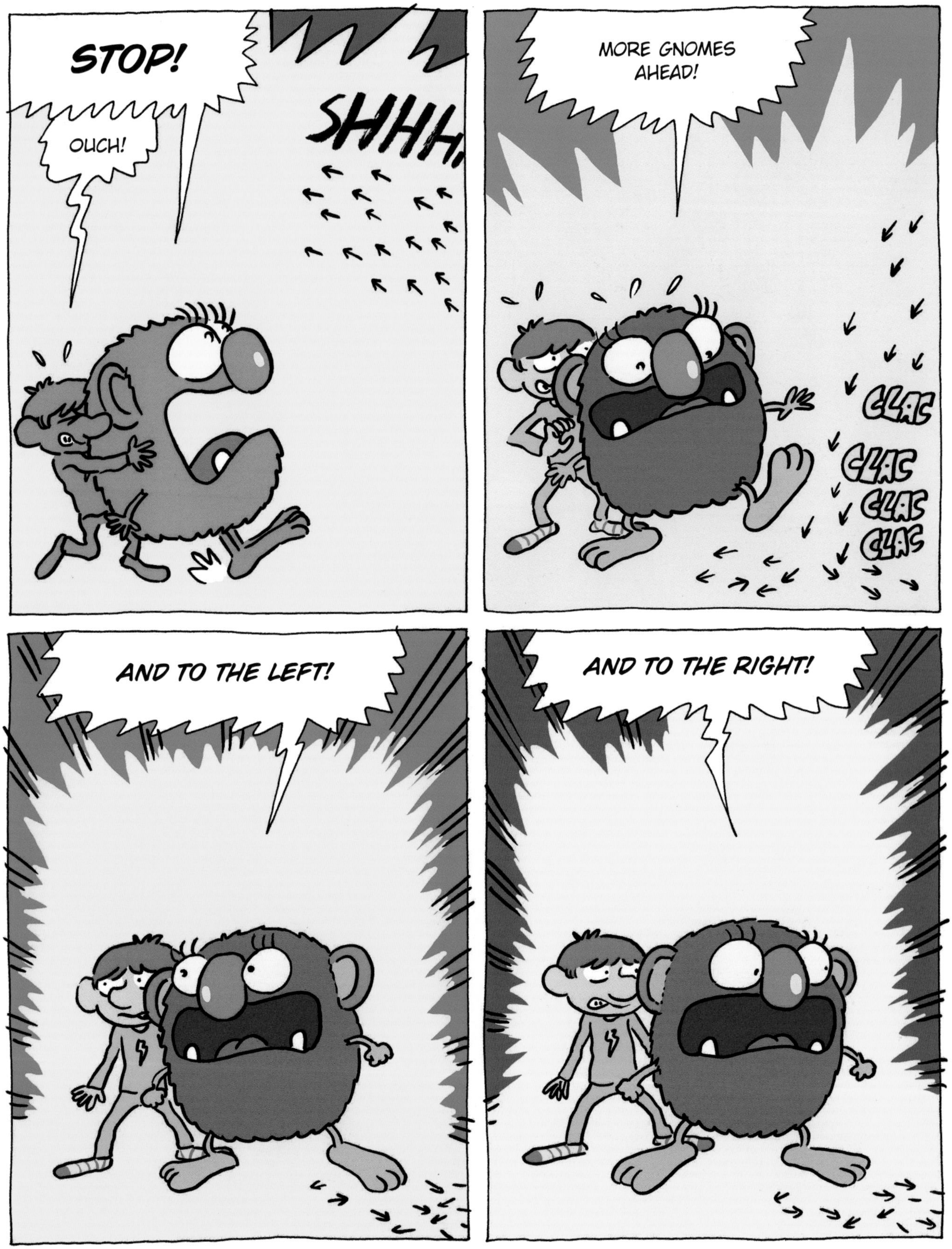

STOP!
OUCH!
SHHH.
MORE GNOMES AHEAD!
CLAC
CLAC
CLAC
CLAC
AND TO THE LEFT!
AND TO THE RIGHT!

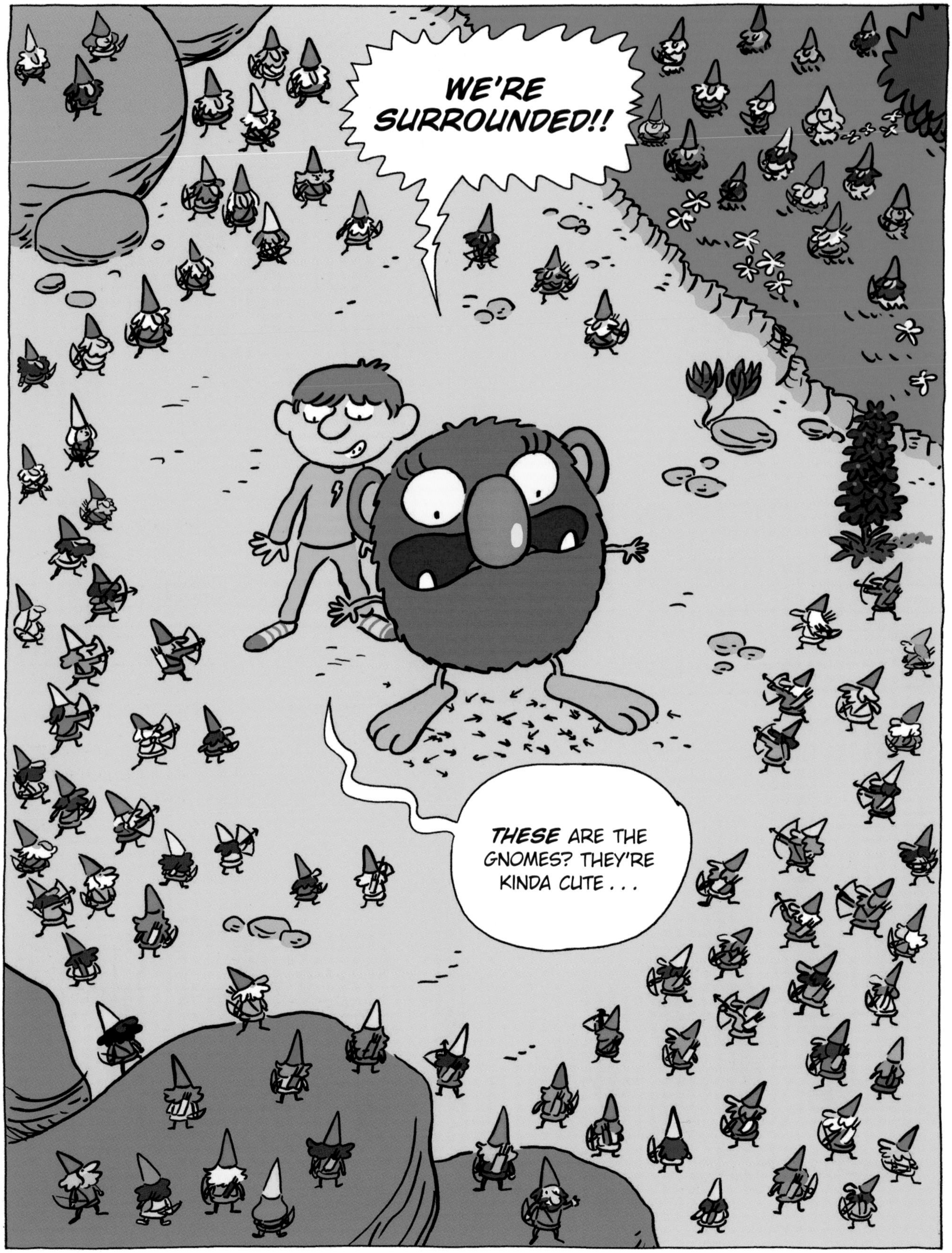
WE'RE SURROUNDED!!
THESE ARE THE GNOMES? THEY'RE KINDA CUTE . . .

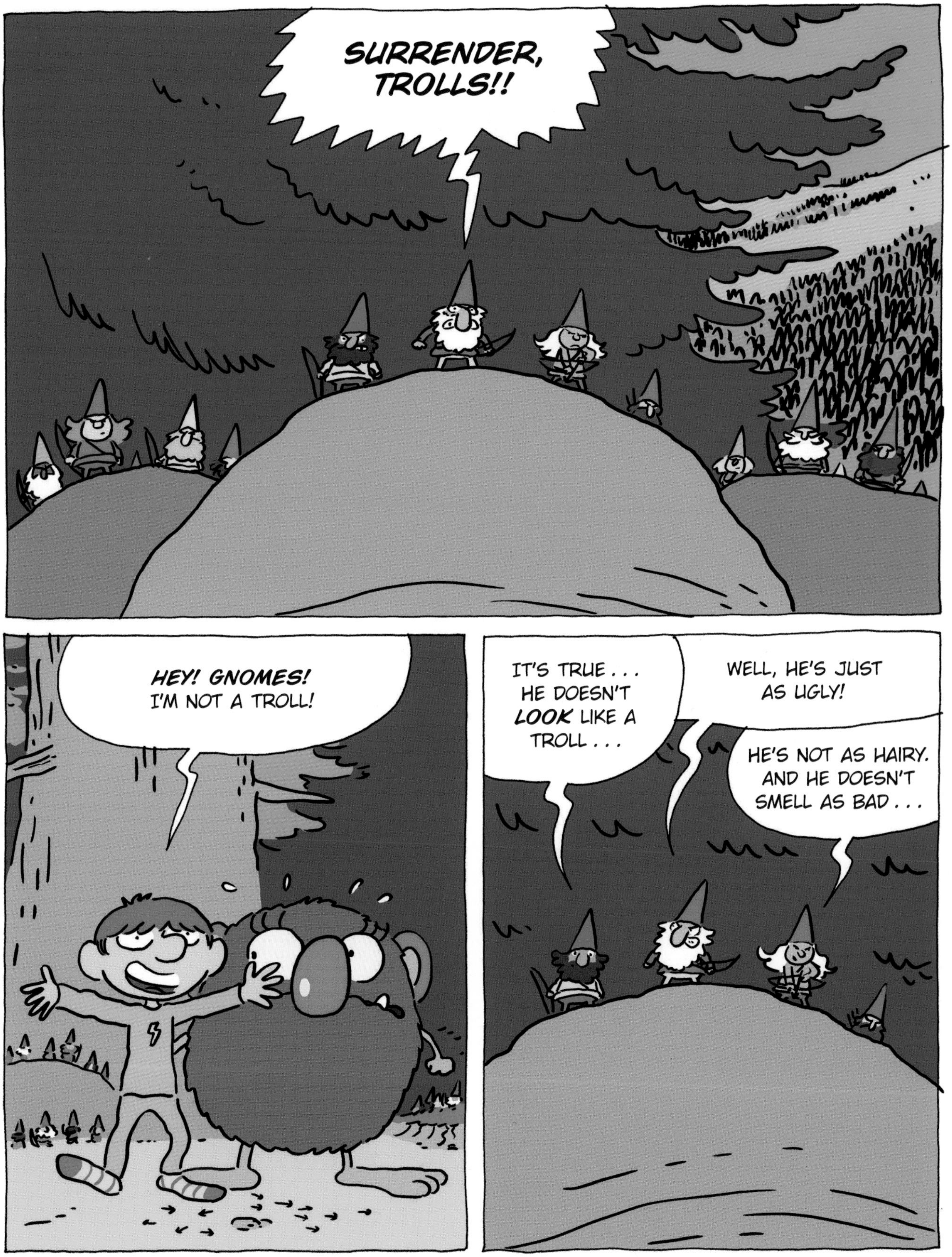
SURRENDER, TROLLS!!
HEY! GNOMES! I'M NOT A TROLL!
IT'S TRUE . . . HE DOESN'T LOOK LIKE A TROLL . . .
WELL, HE'S JUST AS UGLY!
HE'S NOT AS HAIRY. AND HE DOESN'T SMELL AS BAD . . .

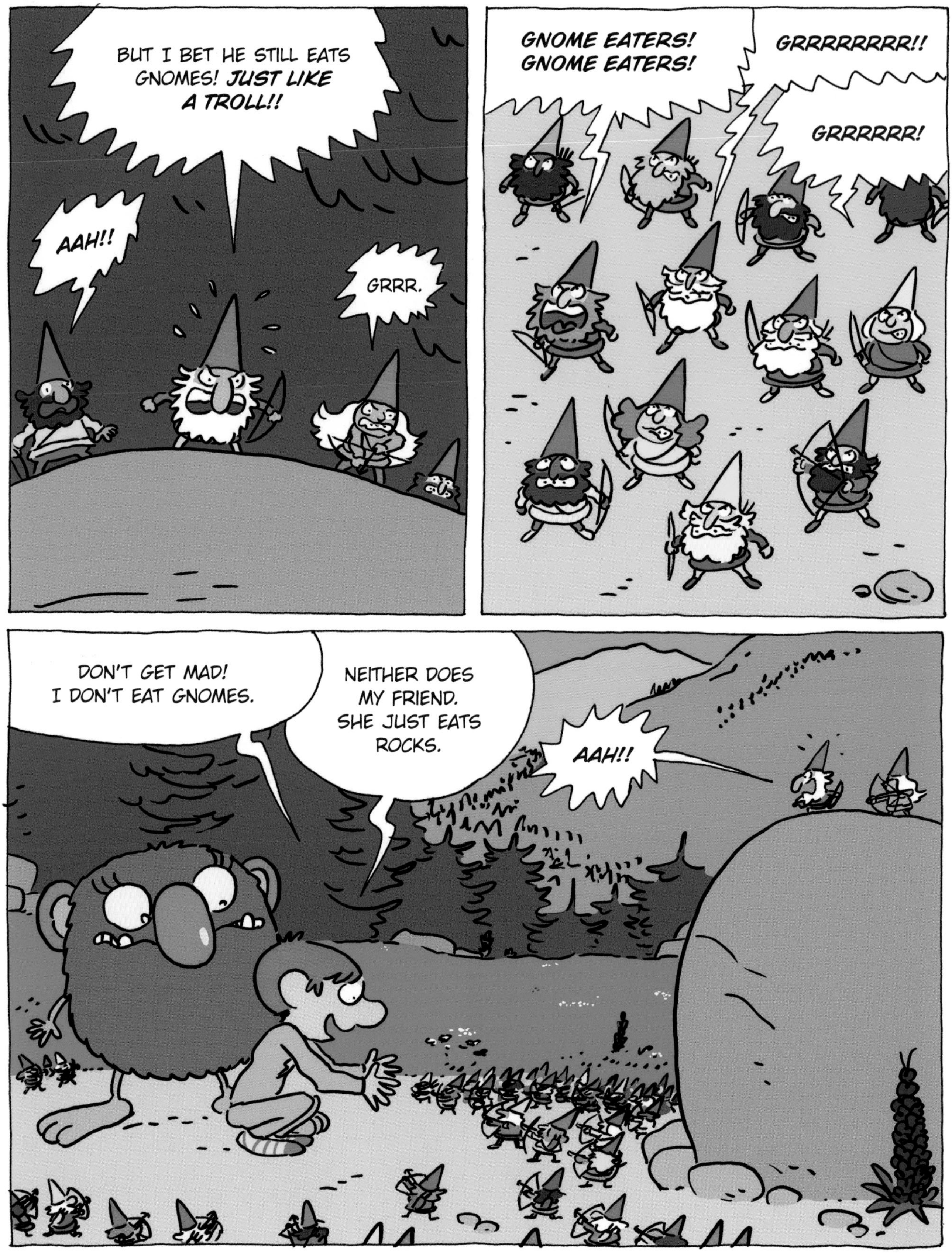

BUT I BET HE STILL EATS GNOMES! JUST LIKE A TROLL!!
AAH!!
GRRR.
GNOME EATERS! GNOME EATERS!
GRRRRRRRR!!
GRRRRRR!
DON'T GET MAD! I DON'T EAT GNOMES.
NEITHER DOES MY FRIEND. SHE JUST EATS ROCKS.
AAH!!

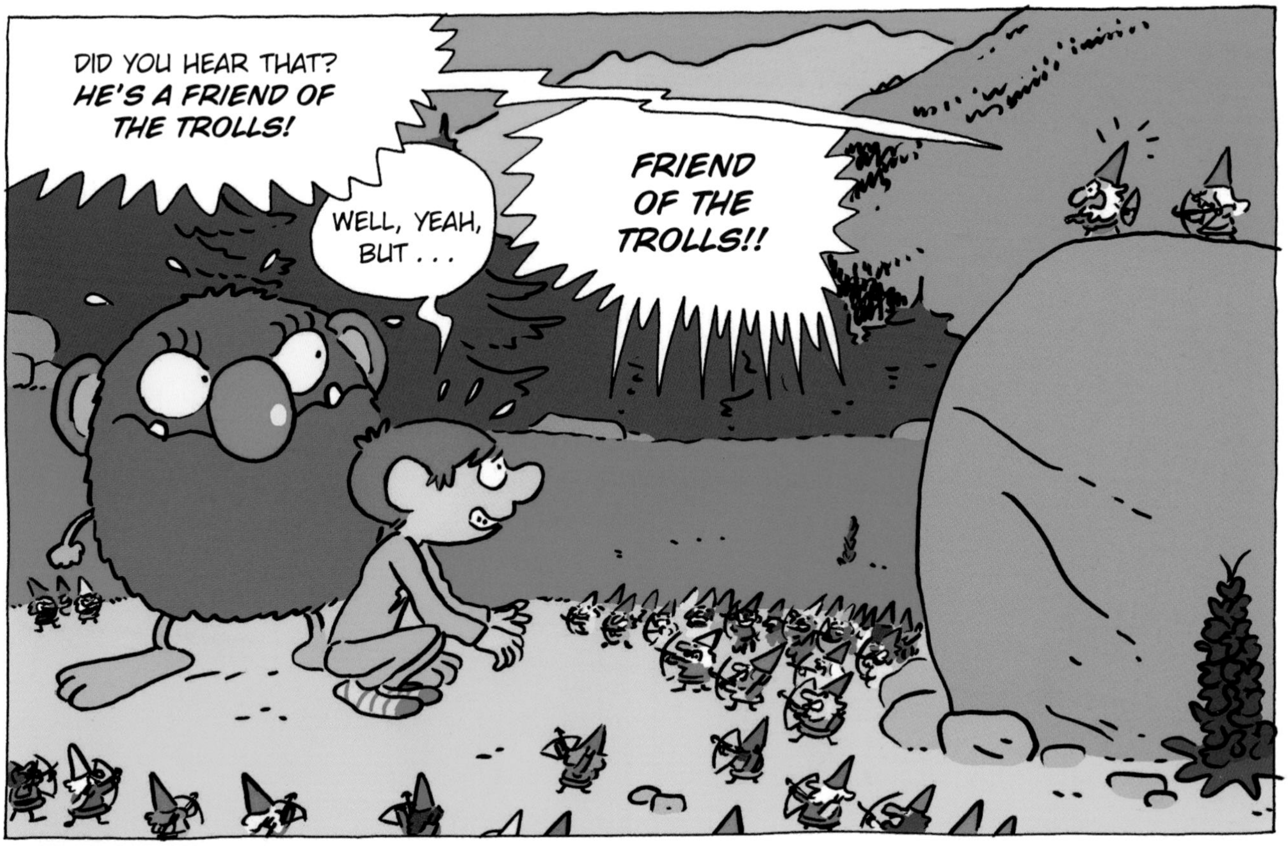
DID YOU HEAR THAT? HE'S A FRIEND OF THE TROLLS!
WELL, YEAH, BUT . . .
FRIEND OF THE TROLLS!!

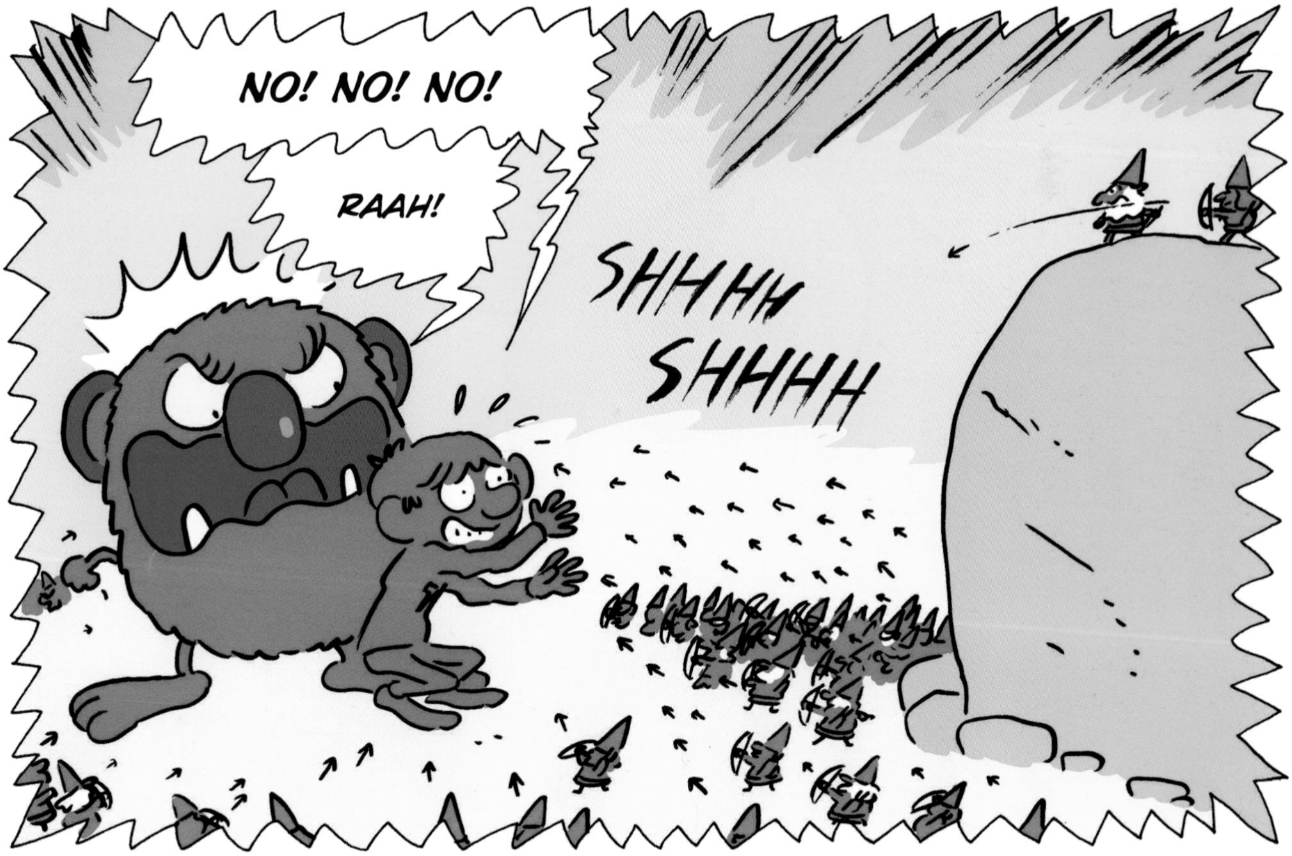
NO! NO! NO!
RAAH!
SHHHH
SHHHH

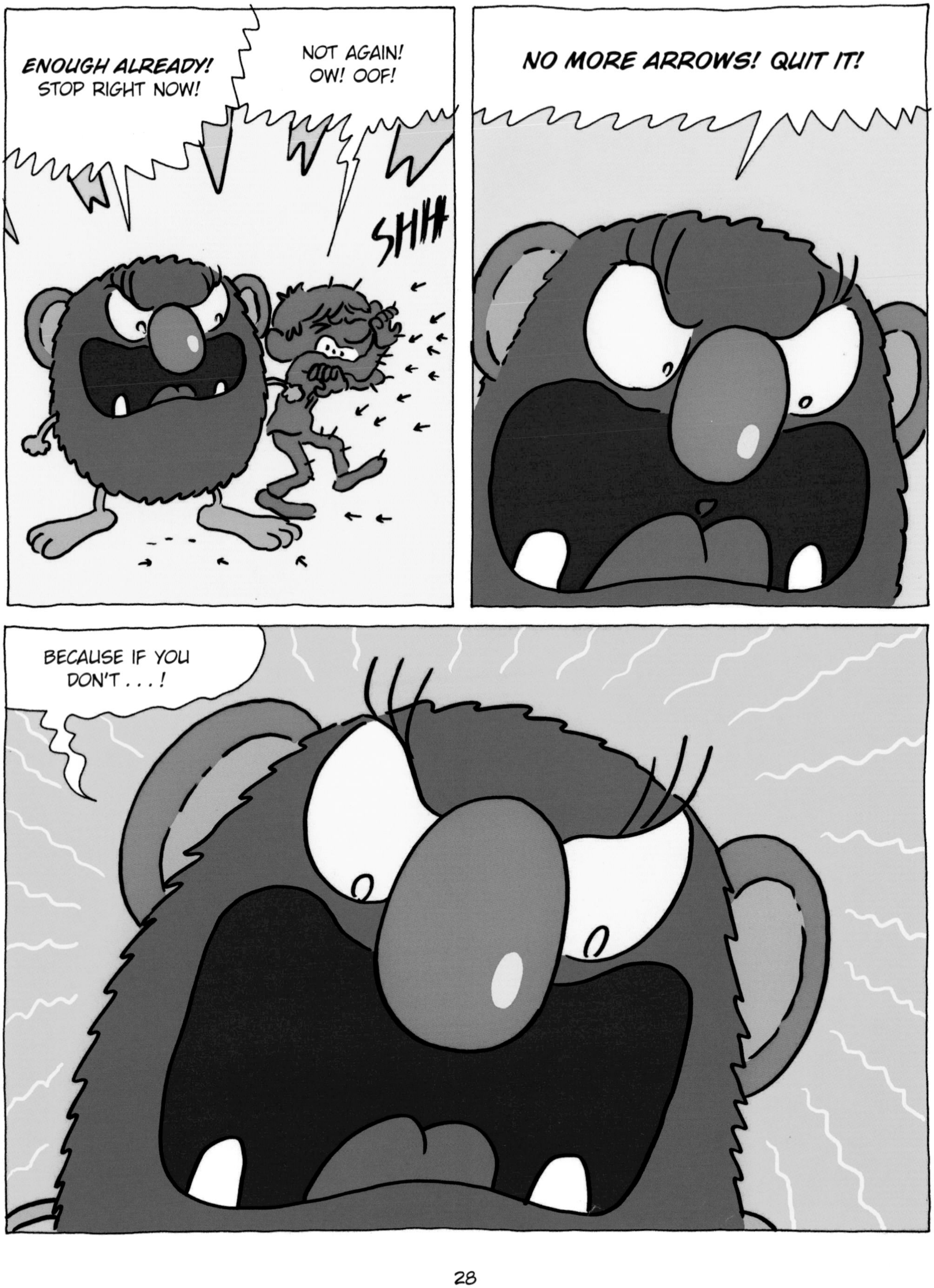
ENOUGH ALREADY! STOP RIGHT NOW!
NOT AGAIN! OW! OOF!
SHHH
NO MORE ARROWS! QUIT IT!
BECAUSE IF YOU DON'T . . . !

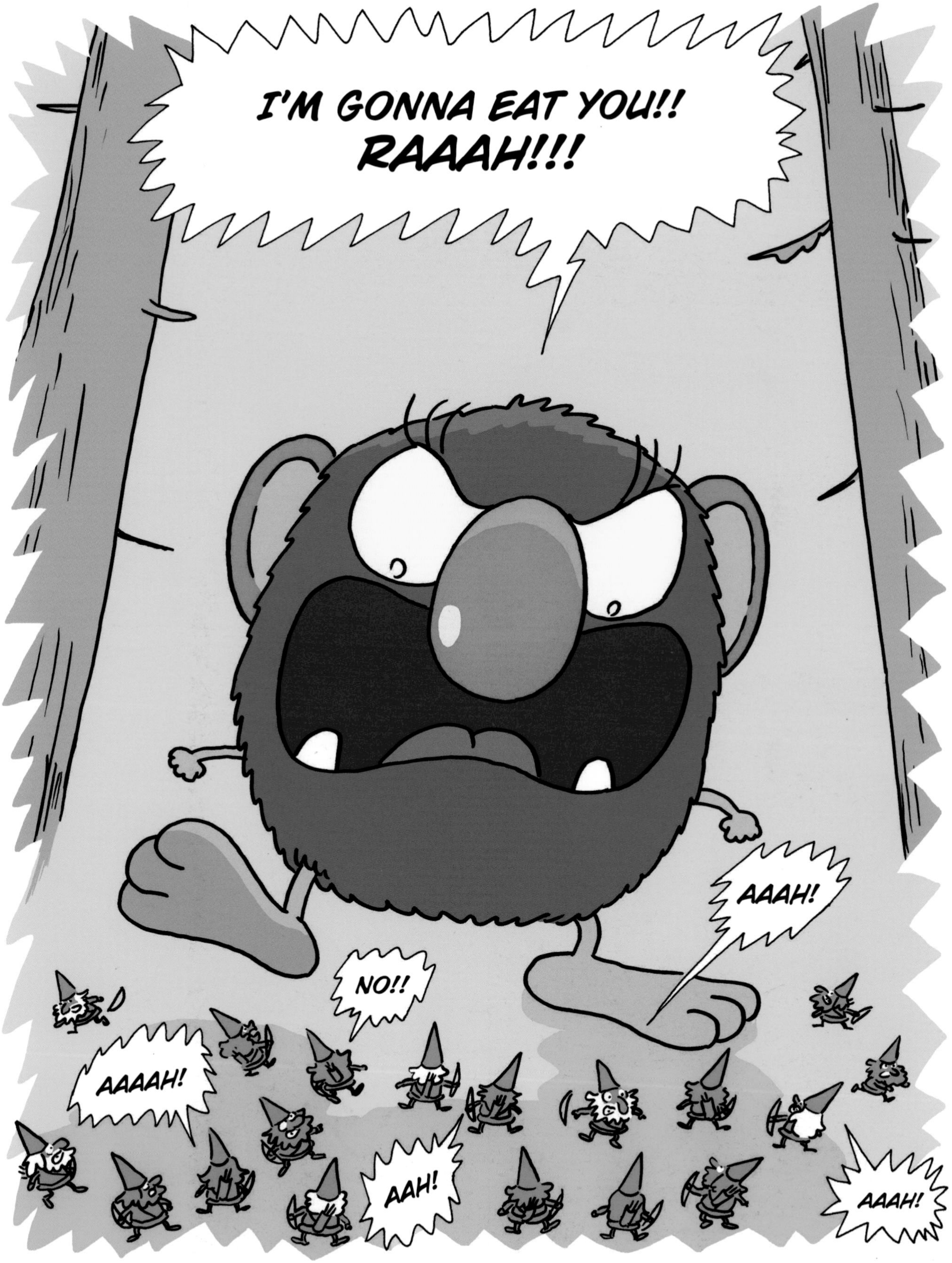
I'M GONNA EAT YOU!!
RAAAH!!!
AAAH!
NO!!
AAAAH!
AAH!
AAAH!

34

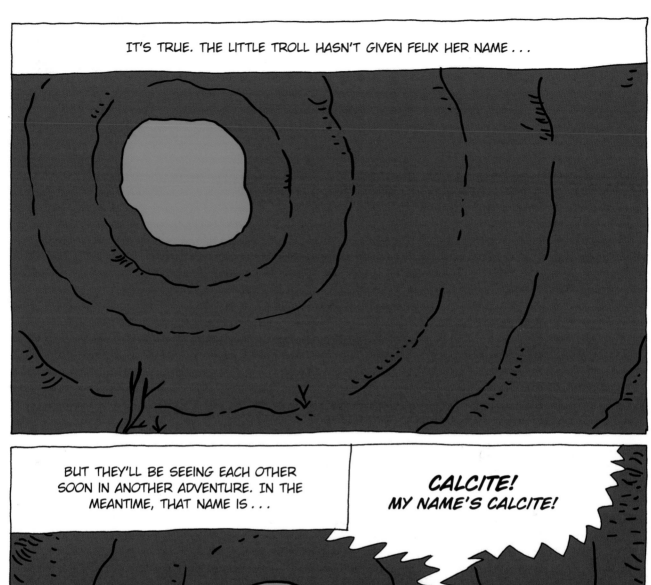

IT'S TRUE. THE LITTLE TROLL HASN'T GIVEN FELIX HER NAME . . .

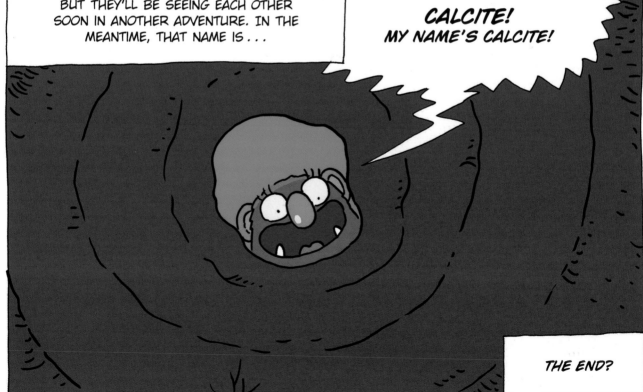

BUT THEY'LL BE SEEING EACH OTHER SOON IN ANOTHER ADVENTURE. IN THE MEANTIME, THAT NAME IS . . .

CALCITE! MY NAME'S CALCITE!

THE END?

FOR A TRULY HAPPY ENDING, AND TO
STOP THE GNOMES FROM HUNTING
ANY MORE TROLLS, FIND SAMSON
THE EXTRA-STRONG GNOME. HE'S
BETWEEN PAGES 24 AND 35.

AND LOOK OUT FOR
THE NEXT ADVENTURE OF

FELIX and CALCITE

BOOK TWO, *NEVER MAKE A GIANT MAD,*
IS COMING SOON!